Lodesville Lawman

Ed Hapgood

A Black Horse Western

ROBERT HALE · LONDON

© Ed Hapgood 2004
First published in Great Britain 2004

ISBN 0 7090 7471 9

Robert Hale Limited
Clerkenwell House
Clerkenwell Green
London EC1R 0HT

Typeset by
Derek Doyle & Associates, Liverpool.
Printed and bound in Great Britain by
Antony Rowe Limited, Wiltshire

Lodesville Lawman

The small, peaceful town of Lodesville is changed forever when five outlaws appear on the horizon. They are waiting to ambush the stage, and they seek a hiding place in Old Tom's gold mine. Other arrivals in the town have a more peaceful agenda, aiming to set up a printing press. Three further newcomers, the Lane brothers, are wanted criminals, intent on blackmail and forgery.

Now the sheriff must wrestle with the growing conflicts, for gunfire is due to shatter the peace of the town. But will his determination and skills be sufficient to overcome the forces of evil and bring peace to Lodesville?

CHAPTER 1

Old Tom didn't hear the approaching riders. For one thing he was too busy panning for gold from the stream that ran outside the cave. For another, having reached the age of seventy, he had become almost completely deaf. The first inkling he had of the approach of the five riders was when his old mare gave a warning whinny.

He glanced up. The riders were now only about fifty yards away. They looked like outlaws. Old Tom hadn't lived all his life prospecting for gold without being able to identify outlaws when he saw them. He quickly reached for his Winchester.

They drew up a few yards away.

'There's no need to shoot us, old-timer,' said the leader. 'We're only passing through.'

'Just keep passing,' said Tom, emphasizing the point by raising his rifle.

'Is there any gold here?' asked another.

'If there is, it's not for the likes of you,' said Tom.

'Is it all right if we water our horses?' demanded the leader. 'We've been riding for some time.'

Tom wasn't happy about the request, but he realized he couldn't very well refuse it. The code of the West demanded that a horse should be properly treated whatever you might think of the person riding it.

'All right. And make it quick.' He again shifted the rifle threateningly.

They dismounted from their horses and led them to the stream. It was obvious from the way the horses were drinking that they had been for some time without water.

The five men wandered around while the horses drank. It was difficult for Tom to watch all five. One of them went into the cave.

'That's far enough,' Tom called after him.

The man turned and started to walk slowly back towards him. Too late Tom realized that one of the others had crept up silently behind him. The last thing he knew was that there was a sudden sharp pain on the back of his head.

Half an hour later the five men who had settled in old Tom's mine soon realized that they hadn't picked the most comfortable place to set up camp. For one thing the mine was damp. Not only was the floor of the mine wet with the stream running through it, but the walls were damp and glistened in the dim light.

'What a place to hole up in,' said one of the them. His name was Samson and the only resemblance to his Biblical namesake was his long hair. For the rest of his appearance he was a weedy character who didn't look as though he had enough strength to push a barn door open. In fact his claim to fame was that he had shot four men – three of them in the back. The fourth he had been forced to kill when he was facing him in a saloon. But that had also been less than a fair fight, since his opponent had been drunk at the time, and had even had difficulty reaching for his gun. Samson's face was to be seen on most sheriffs' offices in the district on the 'wanted' billboard.

'We don't have much choice,' said the biggest of the five, named Tolley. He had worked as a gang-leader, building railroads, until he had had a quarrel with his overseer and had hit him on the head with his shovel, splitting his head open. Since then he had been on the run from the law. Fortunately he had managed to keep out of their clutches until he had joined up with the other four, led by Quail.

Quail himself was the oldest of the gang – he

was at least forty, which for an outlaw was old in the West. Most of them had either been shot or hanged long before they reached that age. Quail owed his longevity partly to luck and partly to careful planning of each robbery they had undertaken. The present venture had been no less carefully planned.

The remaining two, Carl and Linton, were brothers. Carl was short and sturdy while Linton was tall and thin. However they both had plain, pocked faces with lank blond hair. Neither was attractive to the fair sex and in fact they had taken up their life of robbery with violence as an alternative to finding a suitable wife and settling down.

'How long must we stay here?' demanded Samson.

'For two days. Until the stage comes through,' said Quail.

'You're sure the money will be on it?' demanded Carl.

'Positive,' replied Quail. 'Have I ever planned anything yet which has gone wrong?'

'No,' the others agreed.

'What if somebody came here investigating the old man's death?' demanded Tolley.

'Why should they?' answered Samson, sharply. 'I only hit him once on the head. He could easily have hit his head on the roof of the cave and died.'

'Why didn't we go into the town?' demanded Carl.

'Look at us,' said Quail. 'We haven't shaved and washed for a couple of weeks. If we rode into Lodesville we'd stand out as outlaws. The sheriff would soon sign on some deputies and try to round us up.'

'Where's this twenty thousand dollars coming from?' demanded Samson.

'It's being sent from Hawkesville to some town out West,' answered Quail. 'They want it to open a new bank. Only we'll be the bankers.'

The others laughed.

CHAPTER 2

The sheriff of Lodesville, Stan Coombs, sat outside his office. It was the best part of the day. The hot midday sun had begun to slip away to the west a couple of hours ago. The women, many in colourful dresses, had started to come out of their houses and stroll along the sidewalk. Soon the children would be coming out of school. Some of the mothers were already on their way to fetch them from the school which was situated about half a mile outside the town. He surveyed the scene contentedly. He reflected for the hundredth time how lucky he was to be the sheriff of a quiet town like this. He knew from the telegrams he received now and again that the neighbouring town, Hawkesville, was becoming noted for its lawlessness. Here, it was different. A few drunks on a Saturday night, and that was the height of his excitement for the week. Long may it continue to stay like this.

A few minutes later a wagon drew up a short distance further down the street. He watched interestedly as two young men jumped down from it. One of them went to the nearby building, a store which had been empty for some time. He produced a key and went inside. In a few moments he had reappeared. The two removed a tarpaulin which had covered some machine or other. They began to carry the strange object into the building.

Stan wondered about its purpose. It was certainly a large machine since it had taken the two of them all their strength to carry it into the building. They had obviously placed it somewhere convenient and now they had come back out to fetch some more things. Stan couldn't figure out what these were either, except that they were parcels. It took the two young men several visits back to the wagon before they had carried them all to the store. Finally they closed the door of the store behind them.

Maybe he should wander across and find out what the two young men were up to. On the other hand it really wasn't any of his business. He was bound to find out in time. In a small town like Lodesville there were very few secrets. Everybody knew everybody else. True, strangers came into the town from time to time, like the two he had just been watching. But any secrets they might conceal were generally soon revealed. Time was on his side. Things moved slowly in Lodesville. Everything will be revealed in God's time, as the parson was fond of quoting.

Several women passed him. They were on their way to the school. Most of them gave him a greeting or a cheerful smile. One or two of the widows glanced at him longer than the others. They saw a weather-beaten man in his early forties with a pleasant face. He had been sheriff of Lodesville now for seven years and so far none of the eligible women in the town had succeeded in enticing him into their house as a preliminary to further developing their friendship. He had refused each offer courteously, but firmly – leaving the lady in question in no doubt that it would not be worth her repeating the offer.

At that moment one of the young men who had been delivering the strange-looking piece of machinery came out of the store. He glanced up and down the street. He obviously spotted Stan sitting in his usual position outside his office. He crossed the road and came towards him.

'Howdee, Sheriff,' he said, pleasantly, having recognized Stan's star.

He was, as Stan had surmised, a young man still in his twenties. He had an open, friendly face and an infectious smile.

'What can I do for you, son?' demanded Stan.

'I've just come over to introduce myself,' said the young man. 'I'm Luke Price. Me and my brother, David have just arrived in town.'

'I know. I saw you,' said Stan, drily.

'We've come to set up a printing-press here.'

'A printing-press? So that's what you were carrying into the store?'

'That's right. It's a modern press that can print thirty sheets of paper a minute,' said Luke, enthusiastically.

'So what type of thing do you think you'll be printing?' demanded Stan, with interest.

'Anything and everything. Handbills, notices, and above all a weekly paper.'

'A weekly paper? I doubt whether you'll find enough things happening in this town to fill a weekly paper.'

'Oh, you'll be surprised. There are births and deaths for a start. Then there are sales – people want to sell everything from cattle to chicken-feed. Once they see that there's an advantage in advertising they will want to put it in the paper.'

'Well, I hope you'll succeed with your venture. But if you want my opinion you'll go to a bigger town where there's more going on. Why don't you try Hawkesville?'

'We did.' A grim note crept into Luke's voice for the first time. 'But we had to leave town. We

13

were telling too many home truths and we upset too many people.'

'Well if you're after a more quiet life then you've come to the right place,' said Stan.

'I wonder if it will be,' said Luke, sowing the seeds of an element of doubt. Later his remark would turn out to have been prophetic.

CHAPTER 3

At first the weekly *Lodesville News*, as the newspaper was named, caused a considerable stir in the town. In fact the first edition was sold out in the first hour. People came from their farms to buy it. Most of them had never seen a weekly newspaper before and they scanned it eagerly from the first page to the last.

The brothers had produced a professional newspaper with large print for the headlines and smaller print for the stories. To anyone who was interested they explained that they had used Times New Roman print. There was also an excellent drawing in each newspaper. At one time it was the church, another it was of a train, another of the surrounding hills and so on. These weren't the work of the brothers, but the result of a chance meeting in a coffee shop with an older man named Albert. He had expressed his interest in the printing-machine. They had

15

taken him back to their workshop and had shown him how it worked. He had offered to produce woodcuts for the printing press. This meant painstakingly cutting away at a wooden block. It was then inked and pressed on to the paper, producing the printed image.

At first the brothers were dubious about letting Al, as they nicknamed him, produce any drawing this way. In the end, however, they had agreed to give him a trial. The result was that in the first week's paper his drawing of the church was the most praised item in the newspaper.

For several weeks the newspaper flourished. The brothers were making enough profit to buy paper and ink for the following week. True, there was not enough profit to pay Al for his drawings, but he had magnanimously refused any payment, saying that he was more than pleased to see his drawings in the newspaper.

Then the sales of the newspaper began to fall. People would no longer ride in from their farms to buy it on Fridays – the day when it appeared. Children would no longer pay five cents in order to read the exploits of the Robin Hood of the West. In fact his popularity waned after the first couple of productions when the storyline (written by Luke Price) soon lost the interest of the eleven-year-old boys at which it was aimed. The Robin Hood whom Luke described did not live the dangerous life and indulge in the daring exploits of his namesake in England. In fact Luke's Robin Hood's most dangerous exploit was to stop a stage-coach which was being led by runaway horses.

The three contributors to the newspaper were holding their weekly meeting in the coffee house. Judging from the frowns on the usually pleasant faces of the brothers, the meeting was not a very successful one.

'Our numbers are going down,' said David, gloomily. 'Last week we only sold seventy-five copies.'

'When we started three months ago we sold five hundred,' Luke reminded them.

'What we want is a big news item,' stated David.

'I could make my serial Robin Hood of the West more violent,' suggested Luke.

'The parents wouldn't like it,' David pointed out. 'Most of them are keen churchgoers. They say if you put in any more violence it will affect their children.'

'So it looks hopeless,' Luke concluded, with a sigh.

'There must be something we could do to boost our sales,' suggested Al.

'I think we'll have to think of moving on,' stated David. 'As the sheriff said, this town is too quiet. Nothing much happens here.'

'Talking of the sheriff,' said Luke, 'I suppose I'd better take a stroll over to his office to see whether he's got anything interesting to put in the newspaper.'

Stan Coombs was in his usual position outside his office. He waved a welcoming hand at Luke.

'What's new?' asked the sheriff.

'I was going to ask you the same question,' said Luke, taking up a position in the shade near the sheriff's chair.

'I can't think of anything,' said the sheriff, scratching his head. 'Although I suppose from my point of view that no news is good news.'

'Not from where I'm standing,' said Luke, drily.

'There is one snippet,' said the sheriff.

'Anything, however small, will be gratefully received,' said Luke.

'I've got a death to report. It's old Tom.'

'Who's old Tom?' asked a puzzled Luke.

'He owned the old mine a few miles outside the town. It was the mine that originally gave the town its name of Lodesville.'

'So he died? I suppose I can give him a couple of lines in the newspaper. How old was he?'

'Nobody ever knew how old he was. He didn't know himself. He looked about eighty. But I've been here for ten years and he's always looked the same.'

'Did he ever find any gold in his mine?'

'I believe he did. But it was before my time. I seem to remember that he found a few nuggets. But as far as I know he hadn't found anything for the past few years.'

'How did he die?'

'Well it's a bit puzzling.' The sheriff scratched his head. 'He died from a blow on the head, so the doctor says.'

'You mean somebody hit him on the head?' For the first time excitement came into Luke's voice.

'The doctor says it's a possibility. Although it's more likely that he stumbled and hit his head on the roof of the cave. His eyesight wasn't too good.'

'But he could have been hit on the head?' persisted Luke.

'As I said, it's possible. Although I can't see anybody wanting to kill old Tom.'

'Who's the doctor?' demanded Luke.

'Doctor Moore. He lives just outside the town.'

Luke returned to the café with the news about Tom's death.

'I remember seeing him,' supplied Al. 'Although they say he never moved far from his mine.'

'I think I'll find out from the doctor what he thinks caused Tom's death,' said Luke.

'I've got some work to finish on my drawing for the next edition,' said Al, as he too stood up to leave.

CHAPTER 4

In Hawkesville three men were seated around a table in a saloon. If the sheriff had come into the saloon he would have immediately identified them. They were the Lane brothers who were wanted by the law for various crimes including several armed robberies.

However, robberies were the last things that the three were contemplating. They were engrossed in staring at the *Lodesville News*. Eventually the eldest of the brothers, Clint, said:

'It looks very good.'

'It's better than very good, it's excellent,' said the youngest, named Ben.

'Where did you get this newspaper from?' demanded Farley. While the other two had unremarkable faces his was disfigured by a scar on his cheek. It was the result of his face coming into contact with a broken bottle wielded by man in a saloon who had taken umbrage at the way

21

Farley was cheating at cards. His brothers had shot the man but not before Farley had inherited an interesting-looking scar.

'The stage driver brought some copies in from Lodesville,' said Ben. 'He said they can't sell the newspapers, so they're giving them away.'

'It's definitely him,' said Clint. 'There can't be two Al Calders. Especially who can draw like this.'

'We haven't seen him for a couple of years,' said Farley.

'It wasn't our fault that we spent most of that time in jail,' snapped Clint.

'Well anyway, he's our cousin, he should be prepared to do us a favour.'

'If he doesn't we can always persuade him,' said Ben.

The others laughed.

Luke turned up at Doctor Moore's house. The housekeeper showed him into the doctor's study.

The doctor stood up to greet him. He had a round face with white hair and whiskers.

'So you're one of the newspaper men,' said the doctor, as they shook hands.

'One of the struggling newspaper men,' said Luke, as he sat in the armchair the doctor had indicated.

The doctor smiled and offered Luke a drink. When they were both sipping their whiskeys, Luke mentioned the reason for his visit.

'I'd like to put a couple of lines in the newspaper about the miner, Tom, who died recently.'

The doctor stroked his beard thoughtfully.

'There might be more than a couple of lines about his death.'

'What do you mean?' demanded Luke, with sudden interest.

'I don't know what the sheriff told you about his death . . . ?'

'Not a lot. Except that he died from a blow on the head. The sheriff said he could have hit his head on the roof of a cave. Apparently his eyesight wasn't too good.'

'It wasn't that bad that he would knock himself out and kill himself by hitting his head on the roof of one of the caves,' said the doctor, sharply. 'He knew the caves like the back of his hand. He had lived in them for the past ten years.'

'So you don't think his death was an accident?' demanded Luke.

'No, I don't. I told the sheriff of course.'

'What did he say?'

'He looked at the body. He said there was no proof that Tom didn't hit his head on the roof of one of the caves.'

'Who found the body?'

'A cowboy named Dan Blair. He was out riding his pony. The body was a couple of miles outside the town.'

'Wouldn't you have expected his body to be inside the caves?'

'Possibly. Although he might have ridden to the spot where he was found and then collapsed there and died.'

'Did Tom work on his own, or did he have a partner?'

'I never heard of anyone working with him. He was a cantankerous old so-and-so.'

Luke finished his drink. 'Well, thanks for the information.' He stood up. As he was about to leave, he asked, 'Did Tom have any relatives?'

'The sheriff said he had a granddaughter who lives in Hawkesville. He's sent a telegram to the sheriff of Hawkesville asking him whether he knows anything about her.'

'Did Tom own the old mines?'

'It's very unlikely. He couldn't read or write. He wouldn't have had anything to do with any legal documents.'

On the way back to the office Luke mentally wrote Tom's obituary. He wondered whether there was anything else he could add to the doctor's report. Maybe tomorrow he would ride out to the old mines and see whether there was anything else he could find out about Tom's death.

CHAPTER 5

The outlaws had spent one night in Tom's mine. They were all complaining about the conditions.

'I don't want to spend two more nights here,' stated Samson, voicing the opinions of the others.

'The damp has already got into my bones,' said Tolley.

'We haven't got any choice,' said Quail, sharply. 'We've got to keep out of sight until the stage comes along.'

'I thought I heard somebody moving about in the cave,' said Linton.

'Maybe it was the old man's ghost,' said his brother, Carl, with a chuckle.

'I don't think it's funny,' snapped Linton.

'I wonder if they've found the old man's body yet?' said Quail, trying to change the subject from their complaining.

'I expect so,' said Samson. 'We've spotted a

few cowboys riding in the distance. It's likely that one of them has found the body.'

'Why can't one of us go into the town to get some victuals and some whiskey,' suggested Samson. 'One person wouldn't be noticed. Especially if he cleaned himself up.'

'Yes, I suppose that's possible,' said Quail, thoughtfully.

'Well, that lets you out.' Carl addressed the remark to Samson. 'It would take a whole day just for you to get a haircut.'

Samson scowled but didn't rise to the bait.

'I'm the smartest here,' said Tolley. 'I could go into the town and nobody would take any notice of me.'

It was true. Before he had become an outlaw Tolley had been a ladies' man. In fact it was due to his success with the fair sex that he had been forced to adopt his present way of life. A certain married woman had been in the habit of inviting him to her bedroom when her husband was away. However on one particular occasion the husband of the lady in question had arrived home unexpectedly. Tolley had shot him in order to escape from the awkward predicament. The result was Tolley had been forced to become an outlaw.

The others regarded him. It was true. He was undoubtedly the most presentable of the five.

None of them could argue with that.

'All right,' said Quail. 'You can go into town to bring us some victuals and some whiskey.'

'I'll have to shave first,' said Tolley. 'I can't go into town looking like this.'

'You keep away from the women,' said Samson, warningly.

'I've got to smarten up so that I can go into a saloon,' replied Tolley. 'That's reasonable, isn't it?'

'All right. You can shave,' said Quail. 'After that go into town and buy some food.'

While Tolley was shaving the others gave him some advice about what he needed to bring back.

'I want some bottles of beer,' said Carl. 'I can't stand whiskey.'

'Bring me some cakes,' said Linton. 'I don't know when I tasted cakes last.'

'Never mind about that,' said Quail, sharply. 'You just concentrate on getting some bread, beans and whiskey.'

Ten minutes later Tolley set out. He knew that Lodesville was a few miles away. He eagerly anticipated arriving there. He would find a saloon, have a few whiskeys and a meal. Who knew, maybe he would be able to find a young lady with whom he could spend a pleasant hour or so.

Tolley had been riding for about twenty minutes when he spotted a rider coming towards him. It was a young man and to his experienced eye he did not look like a cowboy.

To Tolley's surprise the rider drew up when he had drawn near.

'I wonder if you can help me,' said Luke. 'I'm looking for an old mine. I believe it's called Tom's mine.'

Tolley couldn't believe his ears. Why should a young man, who, from his clothes, was obviously a town-dweller, be searching for the caves where his companions were holed up?

'Well I'm not sure,' said Tolley, playing for time.

Luke said: 'I was told it was in this direction. Maybe it's just a single cave.'

'Tom's mine,' said Tolley, thoughtfully. 'I think I've heard of it.'

His mind was working at lightning speed. If the young man rode up to the mine the chances were he would see the others, who had made no effort to conceal themselves. The rider could spot them from a distance and would instantly wonder what they were doing in old Tom's mine. The chances were he wouldn't stay to find out the answer to the question. He would ride as fast as he could back to Lodesville. He would outpace the outlaws since he was already on a horse, and they would have to saddle their horses to follow him. If the young man arrived in Lodesville before the outlaws could catch up with him then all their best laid plans would be in ruins.

Luke was waiting impatiently for an answer.

'I think I passed a cave about three miles back,' Tolley announced.

'Thanks,' said Luke.

He turned to ride in the direction Tolley had indicated. It was at that moment that the outlaw shot him in the back.

CHAPTER 6

The outlaws were surprised to see Tolley riding back to their hideout less than an hour after he had left it. They were even more surprised to see that he was leading a horse with its rider slumped across the saddle.

'What happened to him?' demanded Quail, when Tolley was within talking distance.

'I had to shoot him,' stated Tolley. 'He was heading for this cave. He would have spotted you lot and headed back to Lodesville. He could have got there before you and notified the sheriff.'

'What would he want coming to this god-forsaken place?' demanded Samson.

'I didn't have a chance to find out. I had to shoot him before he started on his way.'

Quail was examining the body.

'We'll have to get rid of him,' he announced.

'We could hide the body in the cave,' suggested Linton.

'Don't be stupid,' said Quail. 'Somebody is bound to come this way looking for him.'

'Where are we going to hide him then?' demanded Carl, belligerently, coming to the aid of his brother.

'We'll have to take the body somewhere far away. So that it will look as though he was killed, say, going away from the town in another direction.'

'Yes, that's a good idea,' said Tolley, relieved that a solution had been proposed to concealing the killing.

'Two of you can take the body out. Leave him at the other side of the town so that it will confuse the sheriff for the next couple of days.'

'We'll go,' volunteered Carl, quickly.

Quail wasn't too happy about letting the two brothers go. He didn't have much faith in their mental capacities. In fact he believed they were the most stupid of the outlaws. But he didn't see how they could make a mess of this venture.

'All right,' he said, reluctantly. 'Take him as far away as you can. Keep your distance if you see any cowboys.'

'If they saw him slumped across the saddle like this, they'd become suspicious,' said Sampson.

'You two will have to prop him up,' stated Quail. 'We'll tie him up and you two will have to ride close on either side of him.'

They set about fixing a rope around Luke. They left a loop at each end. Then the brothers jumped on their horses and each took hold of an end of the rope.

'All right, you two can go,' stated Quail. He watched them with some misgivings as they began their slow progress.

'What about me?' demanded Tolley. 'Do I still go into Lodesville?'

'I don't see why not,' replied Quail. 'This time, though, make sure you don't kill anybody.'

The others laughed.

In Hawkesville a telegraph boy had delivered a telegram to a saloon singer. Her name was Marie Randal. She was in the saloon where she would be rendering her songs later in the evening. She had never received a telegram before and her initial reaction was that the telegram boy had made a mistake.

'I haven't made a mistake,' protested the lad. 'The sheriff told me to come here. Anyhow your name is on the envelope.' He looked at it to confirm it. 'Marie Randal.'

'Yes, that's me,' said Marie, thoughtfully, as she opened the envelope.

The printed message inside was stark. It read:
YOUR GRANDFATHER, TOM TAMPLIN, DIED YESTERDAY.

She read it a second time. 'It doesn't say

much,' she said, eventually.

The telegraph boy who had been admiring her shapely figure, shrugged.

The owner of the saloon, Steve Young, came from behind the bar to join her.

'Is it bad news?' he demanded.

'My grandfather, who lived in Lodesville, has died,' she informed him.

'What do you want to do about it?' he demanded, tossing the telegraph boy a coin. The lad caught it adroitly.

She hesitated. 'I think I should go to his funeral,' she said at last.

'I suppose I could let you have a few nights off,' agreed Steve. 'Will you want any money?'

By nature he was a generous man and Marie knew that if she asked him for some money he would have given her a handful of dollar bills without thinking twice about it.

'No, thanks, Steve. I've got some money saved up. I'll be all right.'

'All right. Look after yourself. I wouldn't want to lose my star singer.'

'Your only singer,' she retorted as she made her way up the stairs to her room. 'If I hurry I'll just be in time to catch the stage,' she added.

CHAPTER 7

Stan Coombs was seated as usual outside his office. His thoughts, as they had often been during the day, were on old Tom. Was there something odd about his death, or had he just met with an accident? The doctor had said there was more than a slight doubt about the way the old man had died. Of course he could have hit his head on the roof of one of his caves, then managed to get on his horse. He could then have ridden the couple of miles or so to where his body had been found. He then could have fallen off his horse and died. It certainly seemed a reasonable explanation.

Of course there was another possible explanation. Maybe Tom had been on his way to Lodesville. He didn't often come into town, but now and again he was known to come in. On those occasions he would buy a few bottles of whiskey – enough to last him for a few weeks. He would then ride back to his caves, drinking one of the bottles as he went along. On such occasions he would be too drunk to point his horse in the right direction. But it didn't matter, since the old mare knew her way back to the caves blindfolded.

Yes, that explanation was the more likely. Tom had probably been on his way to town when he had been attacked by some outlaw or other. He had hit Tom on the head and the blow had been hard enough to kill him. The theory fitted the facts since no money had been found in the old man's pockets. The outlaw could have robbed him and then gone on his way.

That printer feller – Luke – had decided to investigate the killing further. If Luke had been prepared to listen he could have told him that he was wasting his time. He wouldn't find anything at the caves. But like most youngsters these days, he was impetuous. He was a go-ahead youngster. Well, that wasn't a bad thing. The only trouble was there was nowhere to go for such youngsters in a town like Lodesville. Since the authorities had decided that it wasn't worth building a branch railway line to the town from Hawkesville, then the town would continue to exist in its present half-alive state. The only moment of excitement was when the stage arrived twice a week. In fact it was due at any time. He checked his watch to verify the fact.

It duly turned up about a quarter of an hour late. The stage driver, an old-timer who had been driving a stage way back in the Civil War, pulled up at the livery stable. It was about a couple of hundred yards down the road. But from his vantage point Stan could see who was getting off. He counted three men. They were in suits and were obviously not cowboys. He ran an experienced eye over them. Even from this distance he could see that they wore guns concealed under their jackets. The knowledge made him slightly uneasy. Why should three men, who had obviously arrived together and who looked like businessmen, be carrying guns? He knew the thought was going to worry him until he found out exactly what line of business they were in.

His thoughts were interrupted by the sight of the fourth person who descended from the stage. She was a lady wearing a white dress. He could see that she was quite tall. One of the three men offered her his hand to help her descend from the stage, but she ignored him and jumped down. Stan smiled at the gesture of independence.

The three men turned in the direction of the nearest saloon. The lady in white stood, unde-cided. Then she asked the driver a question. He answered it and pointed in Stan's direction.

She crossed the road and started coming along the sidewalk towards him. Stan found himself wishing that he had shaved that morning. Normally he only shaved every other day – a fact which didn't bother him. But the sight of the cool figure in white approaching him made him think that maybe his appearance wasn't all it might have been.

She stopped a couple of yards away from him.

'You're the sheriff?' She had a husky voice. She also had the pale complexion of somebody who didn't spend much of her time in the sun. She was pretty. Stan took all this in before replying.

'That's right. What can I do for you, Mrs . . . ?'

'Miss. My name is Marie Randal. I've come in answer to the telegram you sent to the sheriff of Hawkesville about my grandfather, Tom.'

For a moment Stan looked at her, nonplussed. Then realization dawned.

'You're related to old Tom?' he stated, incredulously.

'What's so odd about that?' she demanded, crossly.

'I didn't know he had any relatives. I sent the telegram as a matter of routine. I knew he originally came from Hawkesville. It was just a long shot that he might still have a relative living here.'

'Yes, well I'm the long shot,' she replied, tartly. 'I've come to see that he'll be buried properly and to go to his funeral. What can you tell me about his death?'

Stan regarded her thoughtfully. She certainly was pretty. What did the men in Hawkesville think they were doing not marrying such an attractive creature.

'I'm waiting,' she stated, meeting his gaze coolly.

'You'd better come inside. I'll tell you all I know about old Tom.'

CHAPTER 8

The three men who had descended from the stage were having a drink in the bar of the Golden Nugget. It was the most presentable of the six saloons in the town, boasting a balcony where the lodgers could sit outside and watch the people walking or riding along Main Street.

'We may as well stay here for the night,' said the youngest of the three, Ben Lane.

'Yes, it will give us plenty of time to find our beloved cousin,' said his brother, Farley.

The others laughed.

'You only want to stay because you saw that smart blonde getting off the stage here,' said Clint.

'Yes, she was smart, wasn't she?' agreed Ben.

When they had finished their drinks Clint arranged with the saloonkeeper that they should have a couple of rooms for a night.

'I'll have the one room. You two can share the

other,' he informed his brothers.

'What about trying to find Al?' demanded Farley.

'It too late today. We'll try and find out about him and where he lives this evening. We won't ask outright. We don't want to make it too obvious. When we do find him we'll give him a surprise.'

'He probably thinks we're still in jail,' said Clint.

'Yes, he will have a surprise,' said Ben. 'Especially since he was responsible for putting us there in the first place.'

Linton and Carl had carefully circled the town. It had taken them a couple of hours during which they had had to make several detours to avoid going too close to the cowboys who were obviously searching for stray cattle. Eventually Linton announced:

'We'll cut him loose here.'

They were on a wide plateau where there was no sign of any other humans. The only signs of life were the several odd cattle which had strayed up on the plateau and were now looking for some suitable grass to chew. Not that they were having much success since the plateau was mostly sand with only a few grass tufts here and there.

'He's stiffened up,' said Carl, as they cut Luke free.

They let him roll off the horse. The animal, relieved of the weight on its back, copied the cattle in their search for pasture.

The two surveyed the corpse which had landed on its back and was now staring sightlessly up at the sky.

'There's one thing Quail didn't think about,' said Linton.

'What's that?' demanded Carl.

'His money.' Linton pointed at the corpse.

'What about it?' demanded Carl.

'Why should I have a brother who's so stupid?' Linton appealed to the heavens.

'Don't call me stupid,' snarled Carl.

Linton realized that he had gone too far in expressing his opinion of his brother. He knew that Carl had a quick temper, and while he was reasonably sure that he wouldn't draw on him, nevertheless he didn't want to provoke him too far.

'Quail forgot that he has got money on him.' He stated it slowly so that his brother could grasp the significance of the statement.

'How do you know?'

'I could feel the wallet in his pocket when we were tying him up.'

'Then why didn't you tell Quail?'

'Because I have an idea how we can use the money ourselves.'

Carl struggled with the implication of the suggestion. At last he said, 'We can steal it ourselves.'

'Exactly.' There was more than a note of triumph in Linton's voice. Almost a whole octave in fact. His brother had grasped a salient fact without its having to be spelled out to him at least twice.

'Get his wallet,' commanded Linton.

Carl obediently jumped down from his horse and searched inside Luke's jacket. He produced the wallet.

'How much money is in it?' demanded Linton.

Counting wasn't one of Carl's strong points. He took out the bundle of notes and handed them wordlessly to his brother.

Linton flipped through them

'There's twenty-two dollars here,' he announced.

'Hey! That's not bad,' said Carl, enthusiastically. 'If we had that money we could both get drunk.'

Once again Linton turned his gaze to the heavens. This time though he did not appeal to God to save him from stupid brothers.

'That's just what we're going to do,' he stated.

'But Quail would expect us to go straight back,' objected Carl.

'Quail. Quail. Quail. I'm fed up with doing what Quail says,' said Linton, venomously.

Carl was surprised at the anger in his brother's voice.

'So what do you suggest?' he asked, meekly.

'We ride into Lodesville. We'll go into the first saloon we come to. We have a few quiet drinks then we ride back to the cave. Anyhow, we deserve it for getting rid of him for Quail.' He pointed a contemptuous hand at the corpse.

'I'm all for having a few beers.' For the first time there was a smile on Carl's face.

Linton smiled too.

'Right. Let's go into Lodesville and have those beers.'

They both whooped with delight as they kicked their horses into a gallop.

CHAPTER 9

In his office Stan Coombs was still thinking about Marie Randal who had left the room about half an hour earlier. Her perfume had stayed behind after she had left. In fact when she had left there had been a distinct void in the room.

They had had a short conversation but his impression had been that she was a determined lady. He wished he had been able to find out more about her. Although he had told her all he knew about old Tom (which in truth wasn't much), she hadn't divulged a great deal about herself.

He guessed she was a teacher, or some kind of private governess from the way she talked and from her confident manner. In the first place he had thought she was in her early twenties, but having looked at her closely he had revised his opinion and now placed her in her late twenties.

He still couldn't understand why she wasn't married, though. She was definitely the most attractive woman who had been in his office for a while. For a long while in fact.

He had informed her that Tom was due to be buried the day after tomorrow. It was strange that the old man had made strict arrangements about his funeral. A few months back he had told the undertaker, Glyn Keller, that he wanted an oak coffin. It was the dearest of the coffins that were made. He had paid thirty dollars for the coffin and another twenty for the headstone. The inscription was to be: Tom Tamplin, prospector, 1800 – 1883.

When he had told Marie about Tom's funeral arrangements there had been silence in his small office. Eventually, it had been broken by Marie taking out an embroidered handkerchief and blowing her nose. Stan thought he detected a small tear escaping from one of her attractive eyes, which she had quickly disposed of.

'What about the mine?' she demanded at last. 'Did he own that?'

'Not as far as I know,' he told her. 'But I wouldn't swear to it. If there are any legal documents they would be deposited with the town's law firm, Smithson and Clooney. They are the only lawyers in town.'

She had left shortly afterwards. She had proffered her gloved hand for him to shake. For a brief moment he had harboured the absurd notion that he would have liked to hold on to it longer than he did.

His reveries were interrupted by the arrival of David Price. He wore a worried expression on his usually cheerful face.

'Luke hasn't come back,' he announced.

'Hold on, son,' said Stan, evenly. 'Am I supposed to know where he went to?'

'He went to old Tom's mine,' stated David. 'That was over six hours ago. He went at about ten o'clock this morning.'

'Six hours,' said Stan, thoughtfully.

'How long do you think it would take him to reach the mine?' persisted David.

'Let me see. It's about five miles away. If he galloped there he could do it in less than an hour. If he took his time, say an hour and a half.'

'An hour and a half to get there and an hour and a half to come back. That leaves three hours. In that time anything could have happened to him,' said David, sharply.

'I can understand you feeling worried about him, but the chances are there's some innocent explanation.'

'What do you mean?'

'It would have taken him some time to wander round the mine. Then maybe on his way back his horse could have become lame. Maybe he could have ended up having to walk back to town.'

David did some quick mental arithmetic.

'Even if his horse did become lame, he should still have walked into town well over an hour ago.'

Secretly Stan admitted that David was right. The last thing he wanted to do, however, was to show that he, too, was worried. It would add fuel to David's already troubled expression.

'We'll just have to wait and see if he turns up,' said Stan.

'There must be something we can do.' David sounded agitated. 'I think I'll ride out to the mines myself.'

'It's getting late,' Stan pointed out. 'You could get there before darkness sets in, but you'll have to ride back in the dark. You could easily get lost. Then tomorrow we could be out looking for you as well.'

David glanced out through the window as if to confirm the truth of the sheriff's statement. There was no doubt about it, the sun was already low on the horizon.

'If he doesn't turn up tonight, I'll ride out to Tom's mine first thing in the morning,' said Stan.

David turned his attention away from the

window. He nodded slowly.

'I'll ride out with you,' he stated.

'It probably won't be necessary,' said Stan, reassuringly. 'You'll probably find that he's come back already.'

'I hope so,' said David, fervently. 'We came to this town thinking it would be a nice, quiet place to come to.'

'It still is,' Stan assured him.

CHAPTER 10

The bar in the Golden Nugget was beginning to fill up. The Lane brothers were seated at one of the tables watching the regular drinkers as they came in. Each newcomer usually had a friendly word with the barman as he poured their drinks. Most of them ordered a glass of beer and were served from one of the barrels which were placed behind the bar. A few ordered whiskey. Mostly these drank a few whiskeys quite quickly and then went on their way.

'I wonder if she'll come down,' said Ben.

'She's all you've had on your mind ever since we travelled with her on the stage,' said Clint.

'She won't come down here,' said Farley. 'She looks too much of a lady to mix with riffraff like us.'

They all smiled.

'I noticed one thing about her,' said Ben, thoughtfully.

'Only one thing?' said Clint.

This time Farley laughed aloud.

'She didn't have any luggage with her,' said Ben, ignoring the laughter.

'If you remember she seemed in a hurry to catch the stage,' said Clint. 'Maybe she didn't have time to pack any luggage.'

The subject of their conversation was at that moment having a meal in the small dining-room which was reserved for residents. She was the only person in the room. She was already regretting the impulse which had brought her to this place.

True, her instinct to pay her respects to her dead grandfather had been a laudable one, but it had had several drawbacks. In the first place she would have to hang around in this one-horse town for the next couple of days. This was inconvenient, since she had brought no change of clothes with her and very little money to buy any. She had lied to Steve, the owner of the saloon in Hawkesville when she had told him that she had enough money. The reason she had lied was that she didn't want to become obligated to him for giving her additional money on top of her usual wages. She had an uneasy feeling that Steve would at sometime in the future ask for repayment in a form which she wasn't prepared to give. This would inevitably lead to her quitting her post as his singer. She would then have to move on to another saloon. During the past three years she had been forced more than once to carry out this change in her place of work due to the unwelcome attentions of various saloon-keepers in Hawkesville.

She knew she had enough money to pay for her lodgings for two nights, plus a little extra for another meal tomorrow. But the following day she would have to go hungry until she returned to Hawkesville. Well, it wouldn't be the first time, she reflected ruefully.

She finished her meal. She knew she had no choice but to go up to her room and go to bed. It wasn't a very inviting prospect, since the evening was still young. Up in her room she took off her dress, hung it up carefully in the wardrobe and lay on the bed.

She must have dozed off since the next thing she was aware of when she opened her eyes was a familiar sound. It was a piano which was obviously being played in the bar. It was a familiar song, 'Dixie', which she must have sung hundreds of times.

At first she began to hum it, then, when the pianist reached the chorus she was singing out loud.

'I wish I was in Dixie, Hooray! Hooray!'

When she had finished singing she waited for

the explosive outburst of applause which always greeted her when she sang that song. To her surprise the reaction she heard was very muted.

Maybe the singer isn't very good, she decided. Then another thought hit her. Maybe there wasn't a singer in the bar at all. If that were true it could be worth her while finding out.

It only took her a few minutes to put her dress on, tidy her hair and slip down the stairs. She peered into the bar. Her suspicion was confirmed. There was somebody playing the piano, but there was no singer. Here was an opportunity too good to miss.

She walked quickly across to the piano. A few of those standing by the bar glanced at her with surprise. Some of the seated drinkers also glanced up at her as she passed.

'She's come down,' said Ben, excitedly.

Marie had crossed to the piano and was engaged in a low conversation with the pianist. The result was that after a while he forcefully played a few chords on the piano to attract the attention of the drinkers. Their numbers had now increased to around fifty and the pianist had to repeat his treatment on the keys before he achieved a reasonable silence.

He announced that they now had a singer who had come all the way from Hawkesville to entertain them. The announcement was greeted by a chorus of whistles. When they had eventually died down the pianist struck up the opening of Dixie.

Marie began to sing.

I wish I was in the land of cotton,
Old times there are not forgotten.

The audience listened, spellbound. When she finished they broke into rapturous applause. A few of them began to toss coins towards the piano. Soon more of the drinkers followed suit. Marie began to pick the coins up.

'Remember half is for me,' whispered the pianist.

During the next hour Marie went through her repertoire. The owner of the saloon, a middle-aged man named Wicks, beamed with satisfaction at the success of the singer. When she was taking a break he crossed over to the piano.

'That was great,' he said enthusiastically, after introducing himself.

'In Hawkesville where I sing in a saloon I usually finish with another few songs,' she replied.

'That's great. You carry on.'

'I usually also get paid,' she stated.

'Ten dollars for tonight?' suggested Wicks.

'Yes, that'll be fine.'

'Do you intend staying in Lodesville?'

'I'll be here tomorrow. I'll see how things will go after that.'

Even though she was singing in a saloon she always started the second half with the hymn, 'We'll All Gather at the River'. Her next song was 'The Girl I left behind me.' It was while she was in the middle of the song that Stan Coombs walked into the saloon. To say that he was surprised to see who was singing was a massive understatement. He couldn't believe his eyes. The lady who he had assumed was a teacher or governess was merely a saloon singer. In his estimation a saloon singer was only one step up from a prostitute. In many cases the two professions went hand-in-hand. He stood by the door for a few moments taking in the scene.

When she finished her song he walked across to the bar and ordered a glass of beer.

'What do you think of our new singer, Sheriff?' asked Wicks.

'She's quite good,' admitted Stan. 'I didn't know she was a saloon singer though,' he added.

He listened to the rest of Marie's repertoire. Although he didn't like Marie's choice of profession he admitted that she had a good voice. She could also put a song over, as her final song, 'Tie a Yellow Ribbon', proved. The drinkers called for her to sing the chorus again and again. At last she came to an end. The listeners showered the piano with coins to show their appreciation. This time Marie let the pianist pick them up.

She spotted the sheriff standing by the bar and came over to him.

'Hullo, Sheriff. That's thirsty work,' she added.

Stan took the hint and ordered her a whiskey and water. She sipped it and brushed a stray curl back from her perspiring forehead.

'I didn't know you were a saloon singer,' said Stan.

She noticed the disapproval in his voice.

'I wasn't always a saloon singer. When I came to Hawkesville three years ago my fiancée and I were going to set up a small business. But he caught influenza and died. I was left on my own. I didn't have any money. So I started singing in saloons to make ends meet. And somehow I just seemed to have carried on.'

'I see,' replied Stan.

She finished her drink.

'Now if you'll excuse me I'll go up to my room. I'll call to see that lawyer tomorrow to find out whether he knows if old Tom left a will or not. Good-night, Sheriff.'

He watched her as she walked away. She certainly had a nice figure. Maybe in other circumstances, and if she had chosen a more suitable occupation than a saloon singer, he would have been tempted to try to become more acquainted with her. However in his present position of sheriff it wouldn't be wise to become too friendly with her. The women's committee in Lodesville certainly wouldn't approve. And if they disapproved then it followed that their husbands would also hold the same sentiments.

CHAPTER 11

In another saloon at the far end of Main Street, named 'The Last Mile', two other brothers, Linton and Carl were drinking. They had been in the saloon for some time and Carl in particular was showing signs of drunkenness.

'This is the life, brother,' he said, slurring his words as he put his arm around Linton.

Linton shrugged his arm away irritably.

'Make the most of it while the money lasts,' he advised.

'You've got to admit that this is better than living in the cave,' stated Carl.

There was a roaring fire in the fireplace and the brothers were standing in front of it.

'To think that we've got to spend two more nights in the cave,' whined Carl.

'Shh, keep your voice down,' warned his brother.

One of the regular drinkers who was standing nearby had overheard the remark.

'You two look as though you've been living in a cave.' He chuckled. 'You look like the original cavemen.'

Linton scowled but did not rise to the bait. His brother, though, was more belligerent.

'Just watch what you're saying,' he snarled.

'It was only a joke,' said Linton, trying to defuse a situation which was threatening to become ugly.

'I don't like that kind of joke,' snapped Carl. He moved into an open space away from the fire. The implication of the sudden movement wasn't lost on his opponent. His name was Campbell and his was an unremarkable face beneath thinning ginger hair. He worked on a nearby farm and apart from having an occasional drink in the saloon, for his thirty-two years on earth he had led an ordinary life. His one hobby was practicing drawing and shooting his Colt revolver. He believed that he had become very proficient at his hobby, as he termed it. Not that he had ever been able to face anyone in a gunfight to put his belief to the test. Now, however, all that was going to change in the next couple of minutes.

'If you want some action then go ahead,' growled Carl.

The effect of the statement was miraculously to clear the bar of those nearby. The only exception was Linton, who put a restraining hand on his brother's arm.

Carl's reaction was to push his brother away impatiently.

'You keep out of this, broth,' he snapped. 'This is between him and me.'

Campbell mentally summed up the situation. This was what he had been waiting for. Here was his opportunity to prove that all those hours he had spent on perfecting a quick draw had not been wasted. The other farm hands had poured scorn on his wasting his time drawing and firing his gun. Well, here was his chance to prove them wrong. If he killed the ugly guy in front of him he would become an instant hero. The community would look up to him. More important, women would look up to him. His success up to now with the fair sex had been minimal. In fact it was near zero. Of course there had been that episode in the hay with the plain young girl who used to hang around the farm. But when he had boasted of his sexual success to his workmates they had all chimed up that they had had the same experience. This had devalued the whole episode.

He, too had moved into the centre of the floor. The two were now facing each other with about ten yards separating them.

'Why don't I buy you both a drink and we'll forget the whole thing?' Linton made one last effort to bring the confrontation to a peaceful ending.

'This is between him and me,' reiterated Carl. There was a drop of spittle on his lip which he licked off. He was leaning slightly forward with his legs planted firmly apart.

Campbell stared at him. For the first time he began to have doubts. What if the ugly cave dweller opposite him was a seasoned gunslinger? The chances were that he and his brother were outlaws. They had been living in a cave. Maybe prior to that they had been effective outlaws. True, to look at them now you wouldn't think that they were other than a couple of tramps. But one thing he had noticed. Although their clothes were ragged and stained, their holsters were clean and their guns were polished. Maybe he had better accept that drink after all.

He wasn't given a choice. At that moment Carl went for his gun. Campbell followed suit. In that split second he knew he had beaten his opponent to the draw. His triumphant moment didn't last. Before he could level his Colt and shoot

Carl, Linton, who had drawn his own gun with startling rapidity, contemptuously shot him.

CHAPTER 12

When Marie awoke the following morning it took her a few moments to recollect where she was. The realization that she was in a strange bed in a strange bedroom finally surfaced and was accompanied by the thought that she was also in a strange town.

After she had washed in the ice-cold water provided, she sat at the dressing-table combing her long blonde hair. She looked at her face in the mirror. It wasn't too bad for someone who was approaching thirty. There weren't any tell-tale signs of aging. True, it was rather a pale face compared to many of the sunburnt faces that she saw regularly. But she had a naturally pale complexion and this coupled with the fact that she normally spent much of her time in a saloon helped to account for her lack of colour.

On the subject of ages, how old did she think the sheriff would be? Thirty? Thirty-five? Forty?

Well, whatever age, he certainly seemed to be fit. She was used to summing men up quickly. It was a necessity in her line of work. A wrong drink accepted from the wrong person could lead to all sorts of trouble – as she had found out to her cost on more than one occasion. Those times, however, had been when she had first started working as a saloon singer. Now she was almost one hundred per cent certain in her summing-up of men.

The sheriff, she would bet her last dollar, would be a solid, trustworthy member of the community. The sort of person a woman wouldn't mind spending the rest of her life with. Except for one thing. He despised her profession. Oh, yes, despised wasn't too strong a word. She had seen the expression on his face when she had approached him last night. Not to mention the disapproval in his voice.

Well, she probably wouldn't see him again or hear his disapproval. She'd call for a cup of coffee and a bite to eat at one of the coffee houses. Then she'd visit the lawyer to find out whether her grandfather had made a will. Afterwards she'd make the arrangements for his funeral. She'd give one more performance tonight. It would be her swansong. It would definitely be worth it if the audience were as generous as last night. Then tomorrow morning she'd catch the stage back to Hawkesville.

When at last she set foot outside the saloon the sun was already beginning to warm the town. A passing wagon sprayed a cloud of dust in her direction and she was forced to hold her hand over her face to avoid getting some of it in her eyes. As she walked along she became aware of the glances from the people who were already, at this early hour, on the sidewalk. Most of them were women and most of the glances were curious – the townsfolk obviously didn't see too many strangers in town. A few of the women, however, cast envious glances in her direction. She was smartly dressed, while they were wearing comparably shabbier clothes, as became country folk. The only time they would be wearing their smart clothes would be on Sunday when they went to church.

Another reason for their envy was the fact that she was definitely pretty. In fact she cut an arresting figure as she walked along the sidewalk searching for a coffee shop.

She found one at last, and stepped inside the small room. She glanced around for an empty table. There wasn't one. To her surprise, however, she spotted the sheriff seated alone at a corner table. He was staring out through the window deep in thought. She hesitated, then realizing that the seat opposite him was the only spare one, she approached him.

'May I?' she asked.

She had obviously broken into his reverie. He looked up; at first his face was expressionless, then it broke into a smile. She could have sworn that it was genuine and not forced.

'By all means. Here, allow me.' He stood up, walked over to her chair and helped her into it.'

'Thank you,' she said, with surprise. 'That was a very gallant thing to do.'

'We're not exactly hillybillies here,' he said, with a hint of reproof.

'I'm sorry if I implied it.' She smiled at him.

She half-expected a teasing answer in reply. But to her surprise the sheriff's face wore the same serious expression she had seen when she came in. At that moment the waitress came around and she ordered her coffee. She waited until it was brought over before interrupting the sheriff's reverie.

'You seem deep in thought this morning, Sheriff,' she ventured.

'I've got a problem,' he admitted. 'A young man was killed yesterday. Shot in the back in fact.'

She shivered. 'The West would be a lovely place if it weren't for the killings.'

'Oh, they don't happen often in Lodesville. In

fact that was the first one we've had for some time.'

'Hawkesville is a more dangerous town. There must have been half a dozen killings since I've been there.'

The sheriff ignored her comment. He seemed to have gone back into his reverie again. She sipped her coffee. She had intended to order some tortillas, but it had slipped her mind.

Eventually Stan began to speak.

'He was a young man named Luke Price. He and his brother run a newspaper in town. They started up a few months back. At first it quite a success, but lately it hasn't been doing so well.

'Yesterday morning he set out to visit your grandfather's old mine. He thought there might be a story in the way your grandfather died. I told him I thought he was wasting his time, but he was young and keen, and so he went ahead as he had planned.'

'So what happened to him?'

'A cowboy out on the range early this morning found his horse. It was grazing. He also found Luke's body a few yards away. He had been shot in the back.'

Although he had tried to keep his voice even, there was more than a hint of emotion in his last statement.

'I'm sorry.' She impulsively reached over and put her hand on his.

'The thing is, I feel partly responsible for his death. Maybe I should have taken more notice of him and gone with him.'

'If you'd gone with him the same thing could have happened to you. If there are outlaws out there they won't take too much notice whether you're wearing a star or not.'

'Maybe you're right. The strange thing is that his body was found at the other end of town. It wasn't found near the caves.'

'So he wasn't shot because he was going to my grandfather's mine, after all? Maybe he'd changed his mind.'

'That's what I'd have thought. Except that there was another killing last night.'

'Another killing?' She folded her arms and shivered. 'That's two in twenty four hours.'

'This guy was killed in a saloon fight—'

'Not the saloon where I'm staying,' she said, quickly.

'No, it's a saloon at the other end of town. It's called The Last Mile. Well, anyhow the guy that was killed was a local man – he'd worked on one of the ranches for years. It seemed he picked a fight with a couple of strangers. One of them shot him. Then they rode off.'

'So they're probably miles away by now?'

68

'I would definitely think so,' the sheriff said, reassuringly. 'Killers don't usually stay around after they've been involved in a gunfight.'

'So do you think there's any connection between the killing of the newspaperman and the man in the saloon?'

'Well, there could be. We don't know when Luke Price was killed. I'm waiting for the doctor's report, but if he was killed last night he could have been killed by one of the brothers who killed Campbell.'

'He was the man in the saloon?'

'That's right.'

'It all seems to fit. Let's hope, as you say, that the killers are far away by now. What direction would they be taking? Would they be going towards Hawkesville?'

'No, they'd be heading north.'

'That's a relief, anyhow,' she said, with a forced smile.

'I'm sorry to have burdened you with my problems. And I'm sorry if I've made you feel uncomfortable about staying here. The only thing I can say is that the two killers are probably miles away by now.'

'So there's nothing you can do to try to catch them?'

'I've passed their descriptions on to the telegraph office. They'll be sent to all the towns in the territory.' Stan stood up. 'Anyhow, talking to you has helped to make up my mind about one thing.'

'What's that?'

'I've decided to go out and visited your grand-father's mine myself. Maybe the killers had stayed there. One of the men in the saloon where the shooting took place thought he heard mention of the cave. That could only be your grandfather's mine.'

'If you're going out there, take me with you,' said Marie, impulsively.

'I don't know.' Stan hesitated.

'I'd love to see the mine before I go back. Please take me with you.'

Stan's initial impulse was to refuse her plea. Then he glanced down at her. After all, it was probably her mine, he reasoned. That meant that she had every reason to see it.

'Can you ride?'

'I've been riding since I was two.'

'All right. I'll meet you at the livery stable in half an hour. I'm going to see whether the doctor's come back yet so that he can fix the time of the killing.'

'See you at the livery stable,' said Marie. She watched him leave the café. Somehow the thought of being involved in some impending action had reminded her that she was hungry.

She ordered the tortillas and another cup of coffee.

CHAPTER 13

At about the same time the Lane brothers were approaching the newspaper office. It was easily recognizable since Al had erected a large sign outside which stated THE LODESVILLE NEWS. The brothers stopped to admire the sign which also depicted an old mine with a couple of men outside who were obviously panning for gold.

'I bet that Al's work,' said Farley.

'He always was good at drawing,' said Ben.

'Let's go and see if he's inside,' said Clint.

The window at the front had been painted over with white paint which covered three quarters of the window and made it impossible for them to see inside. Clint knocked at the door and pushed it open. At first the figure who was bent over a small block of wood which he was obviously carving didn't look up. The three had filed into the shop before he gave them his full attention. When he did so he dropped the piece of wood and an expression of terror stood out on his face.

'Hullo, Al,' said Farley.

'Hullo, Al,' echoed Clint.

Ben didn't greet him. Instead he picked up the wooden block which Al had dropped. He took out his handkerchief and wiped it carefully. Then he handed it to Al.

'You dropped this, cousin,' he stated.

The look of terror hadn't left Al's face. The brothers were enjoying his discomforture.

'You haven't said hullo,' said Farley, disapprovingly.

'That's not very friendly,' said Clint. He perched himself on the corner of the large flat desk. He picked up one of the different-sized wood-carving-knives which were neatly arranged in a wooden tray. He began to clean his finger nails with it.

'Surprised to see us?' demanded Ben.

Al swallowed. 'Wha – what are you three doing here?' he gasped.

'He wants to know what we're doing here,' said Farley.

'He thinks we're still in jail,' said Clint.

'You know what jail is,' said Ben. 'It's the place where you helped to put us.'

'It – it wasn't my fault,' stammered Al. 'Things

just went wrong with the plan.'

'And you managed to get out in time,' said Clint. This time he stabbed the knife viciously into the desk.

Al's colour, which had drained at the sight of the three visitors, now virtually disappeared as he stared at the knife. The force of the movement made it sway slightly back and forth a few moments before finally coming to rest.

'On your own?' enquired Farley.

'My – my partner is expected in at any time.'

'Partner. What do you know about that?' said Clint. 'He's rich enough to be a partner in the firm.'

'It's not like that,' protested Al. 'I haven't got any money.'

Ben had wandered to the back of the shop where there was a separate room. In it stood the printing-press. He called to the others.

'Come and see this. This is just what we want.'

They all trooped in. The brothers stared at the press with open admiration.

'Does it work?' demanded Farley.

'Of course it does,' retorted Al. 'We print five hundred copies of the *Lodesville News* on it each week.'

Clint touched it gently. He moved his hand reverently over its polished surface.

'This is a beauty,' he announced.

'It's going to make us a fortune,' said Clint.

'You can print anything out on this, can't you?' said Ben.

'Most things,' said Al. There was a touch of pride in his voice.

'Things like false certificates of sales of railway stock?' demanded Farley. He had moved around so that he was now behind Al. The movement was not lost on his cousin.

'I can't do that,' protested Al.

'Can't or won't?' demanded Clint, with an edge to his voice.

'What if I get caught?' demanded Al, with panic in his voice.

'Then we'll leave you to rot in jail,' snarled Farley. 'The same way that you left us.'

'It wasn't my fault that they caught you three selling that false stock,' gasped Al. Farley had now moved closer behind him and was almost breathing down his neck.

'It was your fault that you made a mistake in the false share certificates. You spelt 'Britannia Railway Company' with two 'ns' on some stock and with two 'ts' on others. This made some people very suspicious.'

'They thought that there must be something suspicious about a company who can't spell their own name,' said Farley. So saying he seized Al by the throat. 'The number of times when I was in jail I swore I'd do this to you if I ever came across you again.'

'Don't kill him,' said Clint. 'He can stay alive as long as he agrees to print some more stock for us on this little baby.' He patted the machine affectionately.

Farley, who had began to squeeze Al's neck, reluctantly let go.

'I promise,' gasped Al, rubbing his neck.

At that moment David entered the shop. He came through into the back room. His expression of surprise at seeing three strangers there was quickly erased by Farley.

'We were just admiring your beautiful machine,' he stated, blandly. 'Now that we've seen it we might have some business to put your way.'

CHAPTER 14

Stan was surprised to see that Marie was waiting for him at the livery stable. In his limited experience with women he had always turned up first and then been kept waiting for a while until the woman had put in an appearance. Not only was Marie there but she had already chosen a chestnut mare. She was stroking it and speaking to it quietly as Stan approached.

'This is Pam, ' she introduced the mare. 'Isn't she lovely?' She ran a fond hand over the mare's neck.

Stan smiled.

'I can see you've made her acquaintance already.'

'You know, you should smile more often. You look quite handsome when you smile.'

'I expect you say that to all the men who buy you a drink in your saloon.'

'I see,' she said, bitterly. 'It's going to be like that, is it?'

As soon as he had uttered the words he would have given anything to be able to retract them. Marie had obviously intended to enjoy their ride. It was going to be an adventure for her. She probably didn't get much chance to ride, cooped up as she was in the saloon. And now, straightaway he had poured cold water over the project.

He glanced across at her. She was adjusting her horse's girth. Even though she had her back to him, he could sense the anger in her movements. When she turned towards him it was with a hard face.

'All right, let's go,' she snapped.

They rode side by side down the main street. The sight made the women stare. It was unusual to see the sheriff riding with a woman. Especially one wearing a white frock who looked as though she would be more at home at one of the evening parties one read about which were now becoming popular in the West. She certainly had the poise and figure of a hostess. Another thought struck them. Maybe the sheriff had found a girlfriend at last. It was rumoured that he was over forty and still hadn't settled down. Any man who had reached that age in the West without a wife was a source of gossip and suspicion. Although on the face of it the sheriff appeared to be every inch a man's man, they knew that these things can be deceptive. They all went to church on Sundays and it hadn't escaped their notice that even in the Bible there was more than a hint of men being not quite what they should be. Saul and Jonathan were described as: *Lovely and pleasant in their lives* . . . Which could only mean one thing.

Marie was still seething with indignation. So the sheriff thought she belonged to some lower species of humanity, did he? She had thought they had become quite companionable in the coffee shop. It just went to show how mistaken you could be about some men. She glanced across at him. His face was expressionless. Well if he thought she was going to be the first one to break the silence, he could think again. Hell could freeze over before he'd get another word out of her.

He was regretting the gesture which had resulted in him bringing her along. He knew he had made a mistake with the remark about other men buying her drinks, but it was too late now to retract it. Anyhow, it was true, wasn't it? She was a saloon singer, and everybody knew that the morals of such woman weren't what were generally expected by respectable society. He was aware of the interested gazes which were directed at them. He also realized that the focus of interest was his riding-companion. He stole a quick glance at her. She was a striking-looking woman. Especially with her head held high and that look of unmistakable anger stamped on her face.

They rode out of town. Stan breathed a silent sigh of relief. There was nobody here to watch their uncommunicative progress except the scattered cattle. Marie let her horse break into a light gallop and he followed suit. As she rode Marie began to untie the ribbon from her hair. Soon it was flowing behind her like the horse's mane. He glanced at her. The act of loosening her hair had made her seem younger. She almost seemed girlish. Her expression, too, had changed. The anger had now been replaced with an air of excitement. Her lips were slightly parted and her eyes sparkled. She presented such a perfect picture that Stan found himself glancing at her again and again. Eventually, on one of these occasions, she caught his glance. Her answer was to dismiss it with a disdainful toss of her head.

Stan spied the foothills where the cave was hidden. It was still about a mile ahead. Stan slowed his horse to a trot and Marie was forced to follow suit.

'The caves are in the distance,' he said, pointing.

They approached them slowly. They both scanned the surrounding area for any signs of human activity. But they found none. It was a wild place with large stones scattered around, some larger than humans. Anyone could be concealed behind them. Some of them could even be concealing horses. Not that there was any sign of any at the moment.

The cave was now about a quarter of a mile away. Some of Stan's tension had conveyed itself to Marie. She had dropped back so that they were now riding single file. She noticed that Stan had a broad back. It was a reassuring back, which helped to give a woman some confidence when she was riding through such a desolate place.

Ahead of them the entrance to the cave was quite large. Somehow she had expected a small hole not more than a couple of feet high. But this was much higher. A man could easily go inside without having to bend down. Stan's gaze, too, was fixed on the entrance to the cave. He had visited the site once, several years ago. His impression then had been that it was bleak and desolate. The original impression didn't change. The horses were now splashing through the small stream which ran out of the front of the cave. Here Tom had spent years panning for gold. As far as Stan knew he hadn't found any.

They were both concentrating on the entrance to the cave. It came as a shock when a handful of men stepped from behind the rocks. It was more of a shock to realize that they held guns in their hands.

'Well, well,' said Quail. 'The sheriff has come to visit us.'

'And he's brought a beautiful lady with him,' stated Tolley.

CHAPTER 15

The three brothers had arranged to meet Al in the coffee house during his dinner time. They were seated at a corner table when he entered.

They greeted him with friendly smiles.

'What do you want, cousin?' demanded Farley.

Al, looking distinctly uncomfortable, ordered a bowl of soup.

'I'll pay for it,' said Farley. 'After all, we're partners once again.'

Al, who was breaking up some bread to put in his soup, didn't reply.

'Let's look at it this way,' said Clint. 'We're willing to forget the past.'

'We'll start with a clean slate,' said Farley.

'We're willing to let bygones be bygones,' said Ben.

Al, who had taken a couple of spoonfuls of his soup suddenly pushed it to one side.

'We're not putting you off your dinner, are

we?' demanded Farley, innocently.

'Say what you've got to say and leave me alone,' said Al, sharply.

Clint leaned forward. His face had dropped the mask of amused tolerance. Instead it was hard and threatening. His tones matched it.

'You do as we'll say or the buzzards will be picking your bones clean on the prairie. Do I make myself clear?'

'Yes,' whispered Al.

'I didn't hear it,' said Clint, putting his face closer to Al's.

'I said yes,' said Al, hoarsely.

'That's better.' Clint leaned back in his chair.

'It's quite simple,' said Farley. 'We want you to print a hundred false railway-stock certificates.'

'And this time make sure you spell all the words right,' snapped Ben.

'I couldn't help it. I had to write all those separately,' whined Al.

'But you won't have to do it this time will you?' said Clint. He picked up the chunk of bread from the table and broke off a piece.

'It'll take time,' said Al. 'I'll have to do it without the partner finding out.'

'Of course you'll have the time,' said Farley, pleasantly. 'How does twenty-four hours suit you?'

'I'll want more than that,' said Al, quickly.

'First of all I'll have to make a block. That could take a whole day.'

'How long will it take you to print them out?' demanded Ben.

'Say another day,' said Al.

Clint and Ben glanced enquiringly at Farley. He hesitated for a moment then he nodded.

'All right. We'll meet here in two days' time. You'd better have the share certificates ready. If you haven't . . .' He drew a graphic hand across his throat.

The three stood up.

'Enjoy your meal,' said Clint.

'Get your spelling right this time,' said Farley.

'Your soup's getting cold,' was Ben's parting remark.

David Price was visiting Doctor Moore's house. The housekeeper answered the door.

'Is the doctor in?' asked David.

'Yes, he's just come back,' she replied. 'Come in.'

Doctor Moore had indeed just taken off his coat. He greeted David with a smile and indicated a chair.

'I'd better introduce myself,' began David.

'It's all right,' said the doctor with a smile. 'I know who you are. I know most things that go on in this town. You're the brother of the unfortunate young man who came here a couple of days ago. The one who was killed yesterday.'

'That's right,' said David, tautly.

'I was sorry to find out that he'd died,' said the doctor. 'He seemed a nice feller.'

'He was. One of the best,' choked David.

'Can I offer you a drink?' asked the doctor, gently.

'No, I'll be all right.' David took a deep breath and pulled himself together. At last he said, 'I've come here to find out about Luke's death. The sheriff isn't in his office. Somebody said they had seen him riding out of town with a saloon singer.'

'I didn't know that,' said the doctor, with a puzzled expression. 'So that's why I couldn't find him to tell him that I'd examined your brother's body.'

'What did you find, Doctor?' asked David, trying to keep his voice unemotional.

'He was shot in the back,' replied the other. 'The bullet probably went though his heart.'

'So he died instantly?'

'Yes.'

'And he didn't suffer?'

'No.'

The doctor was relieved that the brother sitting opposite seemed to have accepted the death. His questions were delivered in a normal voice.

'There was something strange about his death, though,' continued the doctor. 'He came here a couple of days ago to see if he could find out anything about old Tom's death.'

'The one who owned the mine?'

'That's right. Well, as you probably know, your brother set out to visit old Tom's cave. Yet when his body was discovered early this morning it was found on the other side of town.'

'On the other side of town?'

'Yes, on the north side.'

'If Luke set out to go to the old mine, what was he doing riding in the opposite direction?' asked David, thoughtfully.

'It's a good question,' said the doctor. 'And one to which I certainly haven't been able to come up with an answer yet.'

'Maybe the sheriff has found out the answer,' suggested David.

'Maybe. Anyhow, we'll have to wait until he comes back from wherever he is before we can find out.'

CHAPTER 16

Stan and Marie had been forced to climb down from their horses. The outlaws were ringed around them.

'What are we going to do with them?' demanded Samson.

'I know what I'd like to do with her,' said Tolley, suggestively.

'We've still got another twenty-four hours before the stage comes through,' said Linton.

'There's only one thing we can do with them,' announced Quail.

'What's that?' demanded Carl.

'Shoot them,' said Quail.

Marie involuntarily moved close to Stan.

'It's the only answer,' continued Quail. 'While this sheriff is alive we won't be safe. Especially after we've robbed the stage.'

'So that's what you intend doing?' said Stan.

'You see. Now that he knows there's no way

that we can let him live.'

'Shooting a sheriff is a serious crime,' said Carl.

'It's no more serious than you shooting a guy in the saloon last night,' snapped Quail.

'He didn't shoot him. I did,' supplied Linton.

'Well, whoever shot him, it's a hanging offence. If you shoot the sheriff and the girl they can't hang you a second time.'

'All right, let's get it over with,' said Samson, irritably.

'Are you volunteering to shoot them,' demanded Quail.

'No, I'm just saying let's get it over with,' said Samson.

'It seems a pity to shoot the girl,' said Tolley.

Marie moved even closer to Stan.

'All right,' said Quail. 'We'll draw straws. The shortest straw has to shoot them.'

'There's no need to shoot her,' protested Stan. 'Let her go. She won't talk. She knows that if she does you'll come for her.'

'How can we come for her if we're hanging from the end of a rope?' snapped Samson.

'We'll draw straws,' repeated Quail. He started looking around for suitable bullrushes to use.

'I'm sorry it had to come to this,' said Stan.

'Well at least it will be quick,' said Marie. 'I've always been afraid of dying a slow death.'

Stan looked down at her.

There was no panic in her voice and she was showing no outward sign of fear. He revised his opinion of her. This was a truly wonderful woman. No other woman he knew would be as calm in these circumstances.

'I'm sorry I made that remark about saloon singers,' he said.

'That's all right. I'm used to it.'

'I'd like to say that you're very brave.'

'Thank you. If I'm to die, then I couldn't have chosen a better person to die with.'

Quail produced the five straws.

'Here we are,' he said. He cut one of them in half and tossed one half away. He held them all in his hand, concealing which one was the shortest. He offered the straws to Samson.

The outlaw hesitated for a long while, then he selected a straw. He held it aloft. It was one of the long ones.

'It's not me,' he announced, unnecessarily.

Quail moved to the next outlaw. It was Carl. He, too, hesitated before choosing one. When he did so, he glanced at it to confirm that it was indeed one of the long ones. Then he too held it aloft.

'It's one of us three,' announced Quail.

'You already know which is the short one,' snapped Linton. 'So it's not going to be fair.'

'You'll pick the next. Then Tolley. If you both pick long straws then I'm bound to have the short one,' explained Quail.

'I suppose that's fair,' said Linton. He selected a straw. Unlike the others he selected a straw quickly and held it up in one movement.

'It's a long one,' he said, triumphantly.

'It's you and me, Tolley,' said Quail.

The outlaw who was so addressed hesitated.

'I don't like this game,' he growled.

'You haven't got any choice,' snapped Quail. 'Pick a straw.'

Tolley looked around at the hard faces of the outlaws. He found no sympathy there. He hesitated for a few moments. Then he grabbed at one of the two remaining straws. There was a collective intake of breath as he held aloft the short straw.

'All right, that's settled,' announced Quail. 'Shoot them.'

Tolley, who had appeared uncomfortable during the straw-drawing contest, now appeared devastated.

'I can't shoot a woman,' he cried. 'It's not in my nature.'

'Whether it's in your nature or not, get on with it,' shouted Linton.

'We all drew the straws. It was a fair contest,' said Carl.

91

'Like the way you two killed that feller last night,' suggested Samson.

'If you want a fair contest with me at any time, say so,' snarled Linton.

Quail, realizing that the discussion was getting out of hand, stepped in.

'All right you lot, calm down,' he said, placatingly. He turned to Tolley. 'Are you going to shoot them, or not?'

'I'll shoot the sheriff, but I won't shoot the girl,' said Tolley, stubbornly.

There was a concerted threatening growl from the other outlaws. Once again Quail stepped in. This time he held up his hand.

'If Tolley won't kill them, we'll kill them another way,' he announced. 'This way it won't be just one person who'll be responsible for their deaths.'

The outlaws, who had been encircling Stan and Marie, instinctively moved a step closer. The threatening movement caused Marie to move even closer to Stan. He put his arm around her.

'That's right,' sneered Quail. 'You two cling together. Because the way you're going to die, you two are going to get buried together.'

CHAPTER 17

When David returned from the doctor's house, he went straight to the office. He was surprised to find that Al was already there. Usually Al took a long dinner hour, which was more like an hour and a half. The brothers hadn't complained, since in the first place they didn't want to upset Al, who was indispensable to their dwindling business. And in the second place they usually took a long dinner hour themselves – often followed by a siesta. The latter habit they had copied from the Mexicans over the border. They had often quipped that the siesta and tortillas were the best two things to have come out of Mexico.

David wasn't only surprised to see Al already working, he was also surprised to see that Al was working with a scowl on his face. Usually Al, like the two of them, enjoyed his work. They all had a joke and a quip as they worked. Indeed it was the happy atmosphere of the three of them working together which had largely been responsible for the fact that they were still working. In all reason they should have stopped working weeks ago. They were now losing so much money that the only sensible choice would have been to close the newspaper down and maybe move on to another town. But by an unspoken agreement they had carried on.

David glanced at Al for a second time. When Al didn't glance up, David coughed.

'There's something we've got to discuss,' he ventured.

This time Al looked up from his carving.

'What's on your mind?' asked Al, coldly.

It wasn't a typical answer. Neither was it a typical attitude. After all, they were all friends. They had worked together now for several months in an amicable atmosphere. Now, it was almost as though Al had distanced himself from him. Maybe it was some sort of reaction to Luke's death. Yes, that could be it. Al had been close to the two of them. They had become almost like three brothers. It was natural therefore that Al should be feeling Luke's death acutely. He, too, knew he would never completely get over it. Maybe in a few months' time the stab of mental pain would get less. But it was going to take a long time. A very long time.

'We've got to discuss what we're going to do about the business now that Luke's dead,' stated David.

He found that the words were easier to say in view of Al's apparent coolness.

'What's there to discuss?' Al held the block he was carving up to the light. He examined it critically.

'Now that Luke's dead there's no way we can keep the business going.'

'Why not?' Al continued carving.

'I would have thought that's obvious.' Luke spat the remark out. He hadn't intended to do so. But Al's attitude was now irritating him so much.

This time Al did glance at David, surprised at the emotion in his voice.

'I told you this morning, I'm sorry about Luke's death. Nobody could be more sorry. We've all been friends together and I've enjoyed working here. That's why I want it to carry on.'

'But we were a team,' protested David. 'It took the three of us to run the business. I'd set up the type. Luke would go out looking for stories or advertisements. We worked as a team. There's no way the two of us can run the business.'

'I've been thinking about that,' replied Al. 'There's one way we could carry on the business.'

'What's that?'

'Well, you know I spend most of the time working on the blocks for the illustrations . . .'

'Yes.'

'Well, we'll cut down on them. There won't be any serial story now that Luke's dead. There won't be any need for me to cut any more blocks. I've already done a few dozen. They are in the cupboard. We'll use the ones I've done over again. This should keep us going for a few months at least.'

'Who's going out collecting the news and advertisements?' demanded David, although he felt he knew the answer already.

'I will,' replied Al. 'I know the district. I've been living here for the past two years. I know most of the people – except the newcomers, of course. I could do Luke's job.'

'I don't know,' replied David, doubtfully.

'It's worth a try,' said Al, enthusiastically. 'I think we owe it to Luke's memory to keep the business going as long as we can.'

David admitted to himself that Al was right. Anyhow, if they did close the business down, what was he going to do? True, he could sell the printing-press and the rest of the stock. But that would be admitting defeat. As Al had said, they owed it to Luke's memory to keep the keep the business going. Al was right.

David held out his hand.

'We'll keep the business going,' he said. 'Let's shake on it.'

They shook hands solemnly.

CHAPTER 18

Quail had indicated that Stan and Marie should go deeper into the cave. They obeyed without demur. Marie wasn't concentrating on what Quail's next movement was going to be. She could only feel relief that for the moment at least their lives had been saved.

Stan thought he knew exactly what Quail intended to do. When he saw the outlaw pull out a few sticks of dynamite from his saddlebag his worst fears were confirmed.

Next Quail motioned to Clint to collect some fairly large rocks. He proceeded to do so. His brother joined him. At Quail's instruction they began to pile the rocks at the corner of the entrance to the cave.

'Are they going to build up the entrance and block us in?' demanded Marie, who hadn't noticed the dynamite.

'Worse than that. They're going to blow up

the entrance and bury us alive,' answered Stan, grimly.

Marie shivered. She found herself staring with new-found fascination as Clint and Linton moved the rocks into place, obeying Quail's barked instructions.

'Can't we make a run for it,' she suggested. She had noticed that all the outlaws were concentrating on the work going on at the entrance of the cave and had seemed to have lost interest in them.

'We won't get fifty yards,' replied Stan. 'They wouldn't shoot us face to face. But they'd have no qualms about shooting us in the back.'

They watched with morbid fascination as the pile of rocks near the corner grew in size. Eventually Quail called a halt.

'Now I want a similar pile of rocks in the other corner,' Quail announced.

While the other pile of rocks was being prepared, Stan turned his attention to Marie. She was staring at the rocks which were being piled up in the corner of the cave as though hypnotized. Quail, observing her fixed gaze said,

'You should be honoured. I was saving these sticks of dynamite for a bank robbery.'

'So you're not going to rob a bank,' said Stan, thoughtfully.

'That was a clever deduction. Actually I might

as well tell you what our next little venture is going to be, since there's no way you'll be able to interfere with my plans – we're going to rob the stage.'

Stan thought quickly. The stage? Yes, of course. The stage that was due in tomorrow would be carrying thousands of pounds' worth of notes and coin. The consignment was intended to start a new bank in the town of Sholton.

'You'll never get away with robbing the stage,' stated Stan.

'Oh, yes we will,' snapped Quail. 'I've planned everything. We're bound to succeed. Shall I tell you why?'

'Let's hear it,' gritted Stan.

'Because we know that they're not going to send any soldiers with the stage,' said Quail, triumphantly. 'They're going to make it appear that it's an ordinary stage, although it'll be carrying twenty thousand dollars.'

'Your information is wrong,' said Stan, hoping to bluff them. 'There will be soldiers coming with the stage.'

'My information is right,' screamed Quail.

Raw anger had appeared on Quail's face. Stan realized at that moment that he was dealing with a madman who could change his character completely in a brief moment.

Quail's outburst had coincided with the appearance of his gun in his hand. It was now pointed at Stan's chest.

'I could shoot you for daring to contradict me,' Quail spat out.

One half of Stan's mind said, let him go ahead. Let him kill me. I'm going to die anyhow. It will be a lingering death inside the cave. Why not make it a quick one now. Then the other half replied. Where there's life, there's hope. Maybe they won't succeed in blocking the entrance properly when they detonate the dynamite. Maybe there will be enough space left to move some of the rocks and try to squeeze out. Then there was the problem of Marie. What would happen to her if Quail shot him? While he was in his present rage, would he shoot her as well?

He glanced down at her. She was staring straight ahead. Her normally pale features looked paler but otherwise there was no expression on her face. Maybe she had already accepted the fact that they were to die soon. Maybe she had some inner strength which helped her to come to terms with their inevitable death.

'Maybe I heard wrong about the soldiers,' said Stan, mildly.

'Yeah.' Quail stared at him for a long time as

though trying to decide whether he was lying or not. Then abruptly he turned to the others. 'Have you finished with those rocks yet?'

'I think so, boss,' said Carl.

Quail went over to examine them. After some moments he grunted with satisfaction. He then proceeded to wedge two sticks of dynamite into the corner of one of the collection of rocks they had built. He then stepped over to the other side of the cave and repeated the process. When he faced the two captives this time it was with a smile on his face.

'If you've got any last prayers, then say them now.' He smirked.

'May you rot in hell,' said Marie.

Quail's face twisted into the look of hatred which Stan recognized. He felt sure that if the outlaw had held his gun in his hand he would have shot Marie on the spot. However, he was holding a box of matches in his hand. His answer was to strike one of the matches and apply it to the short fuse leading out from the dynamite.

'You're the one who'll rot in hell in ten seconds' time,' he screamed.

The first fuse was lit. Quail moved quickly across to the other. From their position inside the cave Stan and Marie could see the glow of the first fuse.

'Come on,' said Stan, urgently. 'Get back as far you can inside the cave.'

The cave floor was cluttered up with rocks and they scrambled hurriedly over them. The outlaws laughed at their ungainly progress. Marie slipped on a wet rock and Stan grabbed her hand to prevent her from falling. The sound of the outlaws' laughter reached them as they plunged further inside the cave. It was soon drowned by the biggest bang they had ever heard in their lives Then came the more terrible sound of rocks crashing around them.

CHAPTER 19

The sound of the explosion was heard in Lodesville.

'It must be thunder,' remarked David.

Al merely grunted.

David, who had paused in the act of setting in print his brother's obituary, frowned with irritation. His companion hadn't been any more forthcoming with words since they had shaken hands on the deal of carrying on with the printing.

In fact David was already wishing he hadn't promised to go ahead with the business. He had realized that his heart wouldn't be in it. Without Luke there would be no fun in it. When they had worked together there had been plenty of laughs. Luke had a dry sense of humour. When he had been out looking for copy he would come back with stories of the families he had met. Some of the stories were quite funny, even hilarious. He and Al had laughed uproariously at them.

It had all contributed to a happy working atmosphere. In fact if it hadn't been for that he was sure the business would have collapsed weeks ago. But with Luke's death everything had changed. True, they could go ahead and struggle to produce a newspaper as Al had suggested. But on second thoughts it didn't seem such a good idea.

He glanced across at Al again. The artist was still working on his block. He wondered what it could be. Perhaps it was something to do with Luke's killing, although he couldn't think of an appropriate illustration for the tragic event. The obvious course of action was to ask Al. But he had seemed so distant and unapproachable since lunch-time that he balked at the prospect.

Of course, there was another alternative. In an hour or so they would be closing the office down for the day. When they did so he could slip back inside after making sure that Al had gone on ahead to the cottage where he was staying. He could then print out the block to find out exactly what was on it. Yes, that's what he could do, since Al was so engrossed in it.

He suddenly remembered that he was due to visit the preacher to make the final arrangements about Luke's funeral. He informed Al that he would be going out for an hour or so. His information was met with an uncommunicative nod of the head.

He was glad to get away from the office. The way Al was behaving, like a Trappist monk, was making him feel more depressed than he already felt.

He found the preacher's house without any difficulty, since it was next to the church. The maid who answered the door invited him in. The preacher, a robust, healthy-looking man in his fifties, who looked as though he was enjoying his life on earth, greeted David with a benevolent smile. On hearing David's name he hastily adjusted his countenance to one of sorrow.

'I was deeply sorry to hear about your brother,' he said, inviting David to sit down in one of the comfortable chairs in his study.

'Thank you. I've come about the funeral.'

'There's one slight problem. Before we discuss it, would you like to partake of a glass of sherry?'

David was about to refuse when he suddenly changed his mind. He might as well have a drink with the preacher. At least it would be better than returning to the office to have to put up with Al's lugubrious countenance.

The preacher poured two generous measures of sherry from a cut-glass decanter. He handed one to David with the declaration:

'I only have a glass of sherry at particular times of sorrow. I find it helps to revive the spirit. Of course prayer does exactly the same thing,' he added hastily. 'But sometimes it can be rather cold kneeling in the church. In addition I find I am becoming rather susceptible to rheumatism. So the sherry provides a pleasant change.'

David smiled. He found that he warmed to the rather unusual preacher. It was nice to be in contact with a friendly human being again.

'The bad news is,' continued the preacher, changing this voice to a sadder note, 'that I won't be able to bury your brother until we find the sheriff.'

'I don't understand,' said David.

'The sheriff must examine the body.' The preacher explained it slowly as though to one his Sunday-school class. 'He must see whether there's any evidence which can help him to identify the killer.'

'And the sheriff hasn't come back yet?'

'Exactly.' The preacher brought his plump hands together in a gesture of pleasure that his pupil had grasped the point under discussion.

'I see.'

'It doesn't present too much of a problem. It only means that your brother will be buried on Friday instead of tomorrow. Now perhaps you'd like to discuss the type of service you would like for your brother.'

David hadn't given the service any thought. He had assumed that Luke would be buried, and that was that. But the preacher was looking at him with an obvious expression of anticipation. It seemed a pity to disappoint him. Anyway, why not have a small service before Luke was finally put to rest?

'I thought we might start with the hymn, "Rock of Ages",' said the preacher.

CHAPTER 20

In the darkness of the cave, Marie was coming to terms with another kind of rock. When the explosion came rocks had fallen down and threatened to crush them. The rocks had not fallen all together but had continued to rain down for several minutes afterwards.

Luckily they had been far enough from the entrance not to be hit or crushed by the first fall of rocks. In fact Marie was secretly congratulating herself that by some miracle they had somehow managed to survive the explosion. True they were now huddled together in the dark. True, too, the air was thick with dust from the explosion which was making her cough intermittently. But they were alive. That was the main thing.

'Are you all right?' demanded Stan, urgently.

'I think so,' replied Marie. 'What about you?'

'I could think of lots of places where I'd rather

be, but at least we're alive,' said Stan.

It was a weird sensation. They were in utter darkness. She couldn't see the walls of the cave. She only knew that they were there. They could be several feet away from them, or they could be at arm's length. At some time in the future they would move from their present position and explore their exact whereabouts. But for a few precious moments they were both content to savour the fact that they were alive.

In fact she was enjoying the sensation of being alive. She had been so convinced when the entrance to the cave fell in that the whole of the cave would collapse. She had expected to find herself crushed under a rock. She had a vivid imagination and the thought of not being able to move under the weight of a huge rock evoked a vivid picture of terror. But here they were. Safe for the present.

Stan's arm was around her. That was quite pleasant, too. In fact, in any other circumstances it would have been extremely pleasant. Their initial spat of disagreement had long been forgotten. She had admired the way he had reacted when the drawing of straws had taken place. He had stood his ground without demur. He had even argued that she should be released and he would sacrifice himself. In that moment she had realised that here was a man she could respect. No, more than that, here was a man that she could love.

Not that there would be any future in that respect. She sighed involuntarily.

Stan reacted to her movement.

'Are you sure you're all right?' he demanded.

'Yes. I just thought I'd rest for a while until the maid brings in the coffee.' Stan chuckled.

The fact that they could share a joke, even in their present predicament, was nice. The future looked black – in more senses than one since she couldn't see anything – but for the moment they were as snug as two fleas in a rug.

It was Stan who broke the spell.

'I think we should see if we can move,' he suggested.

'Which way?' She knew even as she uttered the question that it was a stupid one.

'There's a possibility that the explosion opened up the cave. There might be a way out if we crawl to the back.'

She would willingly have stayed where they were for another half-hour at least. Or even for a few more minutes. There seemed to be enough air for them to breathe comfortably. She knew that was the most important thing about being trapped underground. She also knew that there was a stream somewhere which ran through the length of the cave. If they could find it they would have water – another essential requirement for surviving underground. She was even beginning to distinguish vague shapes now that her eyes were becoming accustomed to the darkness.

'We'll start crawling,' Stan was saying. 'You hang on to my belt.'

She obediently slipped her hand in his belt. She knew that it made sense for them to try to find a way out of the cave before they became too weak to move.

'Are you ready?' Stan asked.

It was strange how sound was different in the cave. There was a faint echo as though the walls were repeating the question.

'Yes, I'm ready,' she replied.

'Right. Let's go,' said Stan.

CHAPTER 21

In Hawkesville the Southern Bank had closed. However there was some activity in the room which was usually designated as the manager's office. In fact, a meeting had been hastily arranged between three men – the bank manager, a representative of the stagecoach company and an army major. The rest of the staff of the bank had gone home after checking that the books had balanced for the day.

'I'll explain why I've called this meeting,' said the bank manager, a handsome, well-dressed man named Enoch Grant. Because he was always so smartly dressed he was referred to by the staff, rather irreverently, as the 'tailor's dummy'. 'As you both know, tomorrow is going to be a very important day in the history of the bank.'

'You want to make sure there are no mistakes in the transfer of the money to Sholton,' said the major. He was dressed in army uniform. His name was Mark Revell, but he always insisted that he be referred to by his army rank.

'Of course. Don't we all,' replied Grant.

The third member of the group, Ted Newbury, was a representative of the Plains Stage Company. He voiced his concern about the proposed journey on the following day.

'I think it's risky going ahead without any escort,' he stated.

'The idea is to make it appear like an ordinary stage run,' explained Grant. 'That way we won't be attracting attention to it. We will be more likely to get the stage through without its being attacked by bandits.' The idea of using the stage without an armed escort had been partly his and so he was going to defend the idea to the last. Of course his chief cashier, James McBride, had also been involved in the original plan. In fact to be honest it was McBride who had suggested the idea. The chief cashier had pointed out that if they could get the money through without an escort the bank would be highly praised by the chiefs in Washington. Being praised by the top brass would mean in effect that he, Enoch Grant, would be receiving the praise. Of course if there were any mistakes, and the stage was indeed attacked, then he could always point out that it had been McBride's idea in the first place.

'I could supply an escort of half a dozen fully

trained cavalrymen,' said the major.

Fully trained cavalrymen indeed, thought Newbury, scornfully. Everybody knew that since the war had ended the cavalry had become a joke. Most of the men who were in it were either discharged criminals or men on the run, either from the law or from their wives – mostly the latter. Some of them would even have difficulty in riding the twenty miles a day that the stage covered.

'If I could have a couple of armed men inside the stage together with somebody riding shot-gun, I'm sure we could cope,' he stated.

Grant had to admit that the idea seemed a good one. The difficulty was that he had already publicly committed himself to transferring the money without an escort. He would lose face if he were to back down now.

'I don't think the two armed men inside the stage would be necessary,' he heard himself say. 'One man riding shotgun would be sufficient to deter any marauding Indians.'

'Surely we're not talking about Indians,' said the major. He knew there were Indians further west who were causing some trouble. But not in this neck of the woods. He had assumed they were talking about bandits.

Newbury, too, poured scorn on the bank manager's suggestion.

'We haven't had any trouble with the stage being attacked by Indians for over a year.'

'That's my point,' said Grant, triumphantly. 'The stage will be in no danger. Nobody will know there will be twenty thousand dollars in notes and coin on it. It will be completely safe.'

'How many people know about the consignment?' demanded the major.

That's a good point, Newbury concurred. He waited for the bank manager's answer.

'Two,' came the reply. 'Myself and my chief cashier, Mr McBride. We put the money in bags ourselves yesterday evening after the rest of the staff had gone home. It took us some time to prepare them, but now everything is ready.'

'You seem to have thought of everything,' admitted the major.

Except what is going to happen if any outlaws attack, thought Newbury, bitterly. What had there been to stop McBride or even Grant himself divulging the details about the consignment to somebody? Then that somebody could, possibly unwittingly, have told a bandit. He was aware that Grant had directed a question towards him.

'At daybreak,' he stated. 'The stage will be ready to start at the first sign of light, tomorrow morning.'

'The money will be on board,' said Grant.

'Kindly arrange for it to be here at five o'clock. Everything has been arranged.'

I wish I felt as confident as he sounded, thought a disgruntled Newbury.

CHAPTER 22

In Lodesville David was trying to come to terms with a startling discovery. After he had left the preacher's house he had called at the coffee house. He had guessed that Al was still busy in the printing-works, so he had decided to kill some time by having a cup of coffee. He reasoned that when he had finished his coffee there would be a good chance that Al would also have finished his work. He would then be able to go into the office and find out what had engrossed Al for the whole of the day. Not only engrossed him but had changed him from a friendly human being into a scowling, uncommunicative one.

While he was drinking his coffee a few of the ladies who were in the coffee house came over to him individually to express their condolences about his brother's death. He accepted their expressions of sympathy politely. He was touched by their gestures of friendliness. He knew none of them personally, since Luke had been the one who had gone out and mingled with the community in his search for news for the newspaper. But he felt that the fact that the ladies had approached him was a tribute to the friendliness of the people of the town.

A few hours before he had debated with Al whether to close the printing-press down and move on to another town. But here the ordinary people of Lodesville were demonstrating their friendliness in no uncertain fashion. At that moment he determined to stay in the town, come what may.

Ten minutes later he entered the now-deserted office. He lit the lamp and went through into the workshop. There, lying on the slab, was the block that Al had been working on all day. He picked it up and examined it. It was impossible to see what exactly it contained, although there seemed to be some reference to dollars on it. He knew that the only way to find out for sure was to print the block.

He set about inking the block. He fixed it in the guides. He put a few sheets of paper in position. Then he pulled the handle to print a sample sheet.

The result staggered him. He had just printed a share certificate for the Britannia Railroad worth 1,000 dollars. There was an indistinguishable signature at the bottom. Al had produced a block which could be printed to sell forged railway stock!

So that's what he had been so busy at all day. It all fitted now. Al had realized that the printing business had no future. Al had then pretended to talk him into keeping the business going knowing that he would be pulling out of it in a few days' time. Not only pulling out of it, but taking several hundred share certificates with him for a non-existent railway company.

What a snake in the grass! What a deceitful, double-dealing scoundrel! And to think that he and Luke had accepted him as a partner. Well, if he thought he could get away with it, he could think again. He held in his hand the proof of Al's double-dealing. The first thing in the morning he would call in at the sheriff's office with the proof. It probably meant that Al would go to jail for a few months. But that would be better than swindling hundreds of small-time farmers out of their savings. Because he had no doubt that was Al's intention. He looked at the share certificate again. It was quite a good replica. There looked to be a couple of places where Al hadn't quite finished. No doubt he intended to come in early the next morning and finish work on the block, probably before he himself came in. Yes, that would be it – he grew quite excited at the idea. Al would have planned to have come in early, since he hadn't been able to finish the block tonight. It was too dark now for him to have continued working.

Probably Al intended coming into the office a couple of hours before their normal opening time. This would give him time to finish off the block and print, say, a hundred share certificates. Then ride out of Lodesville and disappear.

It certainly seemed a good plan. There was only one snag. He, David would also be in the office early. In fact he would be waiting for Al to arrive. When he did he would be able to confront him with his dastardly activity.

CHAPTER 23

Marie was on the verge of despair. What had set out as a promising adventure a long while ago, now looked to become an utter failure. They had crawled for ages. She had clung to Stan's belt and they had crawled over rocks. She had lost count of how many rocks she had crawled over. She had soon grown to hate them, some with jagged edges, which pricked her arms and legs. Her dress had been torn long ago. The only thing which had saved her from the jagged rocks was her petticoat. But now even that had been torn. She knew it was only a matter of time before the rocks found her bare skin and scratched it as they had been doing her hands and arms.

In between feeling sorry for herself she spared a thought for Stan. How was he managing? There had been no communication between them since they had started on their long trek.

She would have liked a kind word or two. It might have helped her to keep going. But she knew it wasn't wise to waste one's breath on useless talking. Breathing was already becoming difficult. She was aware that her heart was racing. She was trying to ration her breathing by taking smaller breaths. She didn't know whether it was working. But it gave her something to concentrate on, instead of constantly thinking about the accursed rocks.

The one minor consolation in this terrible form of progress was that they must be going in the right direction. It was the only ray of hope which she clung to amid the depths of her despair. They were following the stream. It wasn't very deep and now and again she accidentally slipped into it. Far from cursing the arrival of the unexpected wetness, she rejoiced in it. It gave her limbs a blissful feeling of coolness. It helped wash away the perspiration caused by her exertions. Now and again she would flick water over her face and this too was a welcome feeling. It was strange that such an everyday activity as applying water to one's face was magnified until it became a source of unexpected pleasure.

However the water was the only consolation in this journey in hell. She had never given much thought before to whether there was a heaven and a hell. If they existed then this was hell. It fitted, since hell was supposed to be underground and they were underground with a vengeance. She even found herself reciting snatches of long-forgotten lines from the Bible.

Yea, though I walk through the valley of the shadow of death . . .

She couldn't remember any more, but it was strange that she could remember this. If they ever came out alive of this hell-hole she would go to church more often. She had neglected her Sunday visits to church since she had taken up saloon singing. It had seemed to her that somehow the two activities didn't go well together. But she would thank the Lord on her bended knees every Sunday for the rest of her life if they ever emerged alive from this.

Until now they had seemed to be crawling along horizontally, as far as she could tell. However, now the direction of the cave seemed to be changing. They were definitely climbing. Stan turned round on a couple of occasions to take hold of her hand and help her climb over a particularly difficult rock. She appreciated his help but was even more glad of the human contact of his hand. On one occasion she was tempted to hold on to his hand longer than was necessary. She knew it was unreasonable. But all reasonableness had disappeared ages ago. They were existing in a world where nobody had been before. They were breathing air that nobody had breathed before. The thought hit her like a sledgehammer that they were going to die where nobody had died before.

As if to confirm it Stan suddenly gave a groan. She guessed that he had hit his head on one of the rocks which formed the roof of the cave. Worse was to follow when he suddenly collapsed without a further sound.

The only sound that was echoing around the cave was her scream. She had succeeded in grabbing him as he was falling. She had lowered him gently to the floor. She instinctively felt his head to see whether she could find a lump which could signify the cause of his sudden collapse. Yes, there it was. On the front of his head. A distinct lump.

She groped around for the stream. She had found it. She gave a huge sigh of relief. She dipped her hand in the water and pressed it against the lump. As a sponge her hand wasn't too successful. She changed her method. She ripped her petticoat. This was an easy achievement since it was probably already in tatters. This time when she dipped the piece of cloth in the water she found that she had a perfectly acceptable sponge. She began to apply the cold water at regular intervals to the lump on Stan's forehead. Even though, by now, she had accepted the fact that they were going to die, she felt strangely contented, as she held Stan in her arms.

CHAPTER 24

Outside the front of the cave the outlaws were eating a meal of potatoes and beans. The potatoes were being roasted by placing them among the warm embers of the fire and then, when they were ready, stabbing them with sharpened sticks, before hastily removing them. Darkness had set in an hour or so before and so there was no possibility of marauding cowboys accidentally stumbling across their camp.

'To think that tomorrow night we'll be eating a thick, juicy steak in some saloon in town,' said Samson.

'And being accompanied by a desirable woman,' said Tolley.

'We've got a job to do first,' Quail reminded them.

'It should be easy,' said Carl. 'It just means killing the guy who's riding shotgun and helping

127

ourselves to the money. How much did you say it would be?'

'Twenty thousand dollars,' supplied Quail.

'Twenty thousand dollars. Let me see, that's . . .' Carl's powers of mental arithmetic stopped short of dividing by five, 'a lot of money,' he concluded, lamely.

'Four thousand dollars, stupid,' said Samson.

'Who are you calling stupid?' Carl flared up.

'All right, that's enough,' said Quail, placatingly. 'We'll all get some rest. We'll have to be up early in the morning.'

'Where do we intercept the stage?' asked Tolley.

'Here.' Quail drew a mark in the dry earth with his stick. 'This is where we are. Here's Lodesville.' He drew another mark a few feet away. 'Here's where the stage road comes into Lodesville.' He drew a line to indicate the short distance from the camp into the town.

'So we intercept the stage this side of Lodesville,' said Tolley.

'That's right,' said Quail. 'You'll only have a couple of miles to ride. But that doesn't mean to say we don't have to get up early. I'd guess that the stage would start from Hawkesville at the crack of dawn. When it reaches that spot,' he pointed with his stick at the mark in the earth, 'we'll be waiting for it. Now all try and get some rest.'

128

*

David, in fact, found that he couldn't sleep. He had gone to bed after leaving the office, forsaking his usual light supper of bread and cheese. Somehow the events of the day had combined to make him lose his appetite.

In the first place there had been Luke's death. That event in itself would be enough to make him lose his appetite for days. Then on top of that there had been the startling discovery that Al was a crook. Not only was he a crook but he intended using the printing-press to further his activities as a crook. The question was, how did that affect him? In the eyes of the law he was now the sole owner of the printing-press (his dear brother having departed from this earth) so in a sense he would be partly blamed for Al's nefarious plans – if the law ever found out.

Yes, that was the crunch. If the law ever found out. It was therefore up to him to make sure that they didn't discover the truth. He would have to devise a plan of action to prevent them ever discovering that Al intended using the printing-press to print forged railway stock.

The more he thought about it, the more he realized that he didn't know anything about Al. True, he had been an agreeable working companion. True, he was an excellent artist. But outside those two laudable attributes he knew very little else about him. He knew that Al had lived in the town for the past two years but during that time he didn't seem to have made any close friends. Or if he had he had never talked about them. On reflection that fact in itself was strange.

He found he was coming to the unescapable conclusion that Al was not only a crook, but that he had been a crook for some time. He might even have spent some time in jail. He could be a hardened criminal. This led him to another inescapable conclusion. Al could even be a dangerous criminal.

Originally he had intended going into the office at first light to make sure that he was there before Al. He would then confront him about the block he had made for the false share certificates. He had envisaged that his accusation would be enough to make Al destroy the block. Of course it would mean Al leaving the firm. Not only leaving the firm, but probably leaving town as well. This was the mental picture he had formed yesterday. But suppose the course of events turned out to be entirely different. Suppose Al refused to comply with his plan and even threatened him with force to try to carry out his original plan of printing the forged stock. Suppose even that Al had a gun!

It was a possibility. It might be a remote one. But nevertheless he had to consider it. In fact the more he thought about it, the more the possibility became a probability.

In that case there was only one thing for him to do. He rose from his bed and went over to a chest of drawers. In the bottom drawer was something he thought he would never have to use – a Colt revolver. He took it out gingerly. That night he spent some time on an activity which he had also never planned. He cleaned the gun meticulously. For good measure he cleaned Luke's gun as well.

CHAPTER 25

To Marie's huge relief Stan had eventually emitted a groan. It was followed shortly afterwards by the croaked question:

'Where am I?'

'You're towards the back of old Tom's cave. You hit your head on the roof. Lie still for a while.'

Stan groaned again.

'I must have given myself a good bang on the head.'

'I expect you did. You've been unconscious for some time.'

He realized that Marie had her arms around him.

'In any other circumstances I would find this very pleasant.'

'I can see you've fully recovered.' This time instead of putting the damp piece of cloth to his head she put it to his mouth.

He spluttered. 'Hey! That was meant as a compliment.'

'Thank you, kind sir. Let me know when you feel like moving ahead again.'

There was silence for a while. At last Stan said, 'I think I can move without my head splitting into two.'

'Wait a minute,' said Marie, urgently.

'What's the matter?' There was more than a hint of concern in Stan's voice.

'Can't you feel anything?'

'Only your body pressing against mine.'

'If you don't stop that I'll give you another knock on your head. Now concentrate and tell me whether you feel anything.'

Again there was silence for several moments. Then Stan said in an awed whisper:

'I think I can feel it. It's fresh air.'

'Exactly.' Marie couldn't keep the excitement out of her voice.

'It's coming from in front of us.' Stan's voice, too, was bursting with excitement.

'Where there's fresh air there could be a way out,' gasped Marie.

'Come on. Let's go and see,' said Stan, urgently.

They set off again with Marie holding on to his belt. This time there was new-found hope in every movement they made. The fresh air couldn't be too far in front of them, could it? The hope was fuelled by the realization that they were still climbing upwards. Marie prayed that Stan wouldn't bang his head a second time. She knew that already he must have a headache. Any further blow would curtail his chances of reaching the source of the fresh air. And if he failed to go ahead for any reason it followed that she wouldn't proceed further either.

They inched their way forward. Was it her imagination, or was the air getting fresher with each upward push? She peered expectantly ahead, but the cave was still as pitch-dark as it had always been.

Stan, too, was straining his eyes to try to catch a glimpse of the source of the fresh air. His desire to get out of this terrible place had increased a hundredfold with the realization that if he didn't get out, then Marie would also perish in this place. The thought of her succumbing to a slow death in this cave was more than he could bear. It was his fault that she had come in the first place. He could easily have refused to bring her along. Now she could have been happily singing her songs in the saloon. Instead of which they were crawling along like some new species of underground animal.

Of course Quail was the real person to blame.

If he hadn't been determined to kill the two of them at all costs, they wouldn't be in this predicament. If he ever got out alive he swore that he would kill Quail. With his bare hands if necessary. He would swear it on a whole pile of Bibles. He was so engrossed in his hatred for Quail that for a moment he almost missed it. Then, there it was! A pale shaft of light coming from somewhere ahead of them.

'I can see the stars ahead,' he shouted excitedly.

'I can see them, too,' cried Marie.

The stars continued to grow in number as Stan realized that they had come to a wide entrance to the cave. They heaved themselves up the remaining few feet with new purpose and energy. In no time they were lying flat on the grass and gasping for breath.

Marie's reaction was unexpected. She burst into tears.

'It's all right,' said Stan, stroking her hair. 'We're safe now.'

'I know. But I can't help crying.'

Stan held her close. He kissed her tears. He found her lips. What had started as a light comforting kiss soon became a passionate one.

When they broke away Marie said.

'It's all right. The treatment has worked. I've stopped crying now.'

'Perhaps we should try the treatment once more,' said Stan. 'Just in case you start crying again.'

CHAPTER 26

David arrived at the office just as the eastern sky was beginning to lighten. He let himself in. He thought about lighting the lamp, then decided against it. He would wait in the darkened office until Al arrived.

He didn't have to wait long. The *click* of Al's key in the lock told David that his guess about Al turning up early was correct. Al pushed open the door and when he saw David's shadowy figure he gasped.

'What are you doing here?'

'I can ask you the same question,' retorted David.

'I – I've got some work to finish,' Al stammered.

'I know. I saw it,' snapped David.

'You saw what I was working on?' demanded Al, with disbelief.

'I even printed it out,' said David. 'A forged

share certificate for the Britannia Railroad Company – a company which doesn't exist, of course.'

Al sat down. In the shadow David couldn't see the expression on his face. He wondered whether he should draw his gun in case Al was thinking about attacking him.

However he was reassured by the tone of Al's voice.

'I'm sorry to have caused you this trouble.' There was real apology in his remark.

'Why are you doing it? You know you'll probably get caught.'

'It's not my idea. It's my cousins'.'

'What has your cousin got to do with it?'

'You don't understand. There are three cousins. They're in town. They've forced me into printing these fake shares for them.'

'In what way have they forced you?'

'They're outlaws. I got mixed up with them a couple of years back. I was broke. I was drawing instant pictures on street corners to try to get some money. They told me they knew an easier way for me to make money.'

'So you've done this sort of thing before?'

'Yes, but the last time I didn't have a printing-press to print the false share certificates out on. I had to draw them individually by hand. Unfortunately I made a mistake on some of them.'

'What did you do?'

'On some of the certificates I spelled Britannia with one t and two n's. On some others I spelled it with two t's and one n.'

David was glad that Al couldn't see his smile in the semi-darkness.

'So what happened?'

'When they tried to pass them off to the public, one of the prospective buyers spotted the mistake. He told the sheriff and the result was the three ended up behind bars.'

'Were you caught as well?'

'No. I hadn't tried to sell any of the fake stock. I made myself scarce. I ended up here. I thought they wouldn't find me. But they did. Now they're trying to make me do something that I don't want to do.'

'Why don't you go to the sheriff?'

'You've seen the sheriff. He's too lazy to get out of his chair. Anyhow they've threatened that if I don't print the share certificates for them, they'll kill me.'

'They wouldn't do that, would they?' demanded David, aghast.

'It isn't an idle threat,' said Al, grimly.

There was a long silence. David was digesting Al's statement. If his three cousins were killers it was possible that they had been responsible for Luke's killing. The fact that Luke's body had been found on the opposite side of the town to Tom's cave disproved the theory that he had intended going in that direction. For some reason or other he had changed his mind. It had resulted in him getting shot. The three cousins were known killers. It was quite reasonable that one of them had shot him.

'What do you intend to do now?'

'There's only one thing I can do. Get on my horse and try to get as far away from here as possible.'

'They'll catch up with you in the end.'

'I know. But maybe I'll have another year's freedom before they do.'

Their discussion was interrupted by somebody knocking at the door. Al motioned David to stay silent.

The knocking continued. Al still held up his hand. Eventually a voice said,

'Come on, Al. Open up. We know you're inside.'

'One of them must have been watching,' Al whispered.

'We saw you and your companion go inside.' The voice confirmed Al's surmise. 'Let us in, or we'll shoot the lock off the door.'

David, although finding himself in unusual situation, did not panic. His mind raced as he tried to envisage the possible events should Al open the door. There was no doubt that both of them would be in a perilous position. Once Al had printed the false shares his own life would be forfeit, since he would be under obligation to inform the law. And not only would Al's life be forfeit, but also his own. He would be a witness to them receiving the false share certificates.

'I'm going to count up to three,' said the voice. 'When I reach three I'm going to shoot the lock off. If you think the sheriff is going to defend you then you are mistaken. The sheriff has disappeared so there's no lawman in the town.'

David came to a decision.

'Can you use a gun?' he whispered.

'Yes, I've used one before,' whispered Al.

David produced Luke's gun and handed it to Al. The person on the other side of the door had already started counting. David produced his own gun. He motioned to Al to stand to one side of the door while he covered the other.

'Three!' shouted the voice. It was followed by a burst of gunfire as the lock was shattered.

CHAPTER 27

On the mountainside above Tom's cave a few hours earlier Marie and Tom were whispering too. But it was the kind of whisper that lovers have used throughout the ages.

'I didn't know,' said Tom.

'That I was a virgin? Not all saloon singers are loose women you know.'

'I'm sorry,' said Tom.

Marie put her hand on his lips.

'Half an hour ago I thought I was going to die. Just be grateful that we're alive.'

'I am. I can't tell you how grateful.'

Marie kissed him. When they broke apart, he said:

'I suppose we'd better move.'

'If we don't I'm going to freeze to death.'

'It's a long walk to Lodesville,' he said, thoughtfully.

'It can't be compared to crawling through that cave.'

'I was wondering whether we can get a horse.'

'There can't be too many of them wandering around here in the middle of the night.'

'No, but the outlaws have got our horses. Maybe we can get hold of one of them.'

'It's too dangerous,' said Marie, urgently. 'I'd rather walk to Lodesville.'

'Anyhow, we'll creep down towards the front of the cave,' said Stan. 'Just to see how the land lies.'

Marie, although far from enamoured of the idea, was nevertheless glad to be moving. She had started to shiver, although she tried to conceal her involuntary movements from Stan.

Stan started to lead the way down the mountain. There was enough light from a thin moon and the stars to make sure that they didn't fall. They proceeded cautiously. Stan wondered whether the outlaws had posted a look-out. He wouldn't have thought so. They would have assumed that they were one hundred per cent safe from any human being. Their only possible problem would be with wild animals. But their fire would be a guarantee to keep them away.

In fact it was the outlaw's fire which first gave Stan the indication that their camp was not too far ahead. It was about a quarter of a mile away to their left. They had both involuntarily stopped when they had glimpsed the fire.

Their initial supposition had been that everybody was asleep. Stan voiced their impression.

'I don't think they've posted a look-out.'

'I can't see anybody, either,' whispered Marie.

'We might be in luck with the horses,' said Stan. 'They're between us and the camp.'

A group of horses were indeed grazing where Stan had indicated. They had wandered some distance from the camp in search of suitable grass. Stan spotted his white stallion among the horses.

They crept closer to the horses. At last they were only about a hundred yards away. Stan gave a low whistle.

The stallion picked up it ears. In response to Stan's second whistle the horse began to trot obediently towards them. Marie held her breath. Would one of the outlaws have heard Stan's whistle?

The stallion came nearer. What had appeared to be just a white blur a minute or so ago now had a definite shape. Stan held out his hand. The horse, having hesitated for a few moments to ascertain whether the person in front of him really was Stan, came forward obediently. It stood while Stan stroked its neck.

'Have you ever ridden bareback?' Stan whispered.

'Not since I was a young girl,' replied Marie.

'Just hang on to me,' said Stan.

He jumped up on the stallion. He reached down to take hold of Marie's hand and haul her up behind him. They began to move slowly away from the outlaw's camp. When they were a short distance away Stan thought he heard a cry behind him. On the other hand it could easily have been the cry of a wild animal.

'Home, James,' he said, letting the horse break into a gallop.

It was with enormous relief that they eventually reached Lodesville. Marie was so exhausted that on a couple of occasions she had almost lost her grip on Stan. However, both times she had recovered in time to renew her hold on him.

The town was deserted as would be expected in the middle of the night. Stan rode down Main Street and drew up outside his house. He slid off the horse and held out his arms for Marie. She thankfully jumped into them.

Five minutes later she even more thankfully jumped into Stan's inviting bed. She had undressed rapidly when Stan had led her up to his bedroom. Stan had turned his head away while she had undressed.

'You can look if you like,' she informed him. 'Anyhow you touched most of my body when we were up on the mountainside.'

He stole a quick glance before she slid into bed. It confirmed his impression that she had a shapely figure.

She patted the bed invitingly.

'Aren't you going to get in, too?'

'I'd love to. But there's something I've got to do first.'

'I know.' She sat up in bed. The bedclothes had dropped away from her shoulders. 'Come here.'

He obeyed. She put her arms around him and give him a lingering kiss. When after long moments, they broke apart, she said:

'Get the bastards.'

CHAPTER 28

If Stan had stayed with Marie no doubt he would have heard the sound of gunfire a couple of hours later as Clint shot the lock off the door of the printing-office. Whether he would have been in time to get involved in the gunfight that ensued was open to speculation.

Clint shot the lock off and as the door swung on its hinges he dived into the office. His first mistake was not making sure that there were no guns in the hands of the occupants. He did not make a second mistake since Al calmly shot him as soon as he appeared.

'One down, two to go,' announced Al.

David was amazed at Al's coolness. Would he be as cool when it came to his turn to kill an outlaw?

'They've killed Clint.' The air of disbelief was apparent in the voice of one of the cousins who was outside.

'That's Ben,' Al informed David, as he thumbed more bullets into the empty chambers of his Colt.

David realized that Al was not only coping with the situation very effectively, he even seemed to be enjoying it. David took some consolation from that discovery. Well, at least the odds were now even. It was two against two. The question was, what did the two who were outside intend doing next?

'Just toss out the certificates that you've printed,' Ben called out. 'We'll just ride away. We won't bother you again.'

It sounded a reasonable suggestion, thought David. The only snag was that Al hadn't finished the block. So there was no way he could print them out.

'Come in and get them,' called out Al.

What was he doing? David asked himself with growing panic. If the two came in there would be more shooting. That meant more bullets flying around. It could also mean that one of them could find an innocent target. The innocent target being himself.

'Let them go away,' he pleaded with Al.

'You don't understand,' Al replied urgently. 'They'll never go away. Not until they've killed the both of us.'

'The sheriff must have heard the shooting. He

should be along soon,' said David.

His hopes were dashed by Ben's next remark.

'The sheriff rode off some time ago. You'll get no help from him.'

'There'll be others who'll come to help us.' David was clutching at straws.

'Nobody will stick their necks out for us,' Al stated, positively.

David digested the remark. If it were true then the two of them didn't have any alternative but to wait for the outlaws' next move. He reminded himself that they had probably been responsible for Luke's death. It gave him strength to make the outlaws pay for their deeds.

'Sh!' Al held up a warning finger.

David hadn't heard anything. Nevertheless he held his breath as he waited for the outlaws' next move.

It didn't take long to come. There was a sudden hail of bullets as the outlaws opened fire. The bullets were fired aimlessly into the office, but their intention was to force David and Al to keep their heads down. David, from the shelter of his table needed no second warning. He ducked almost down to the floor. Too late he realized that the outlaws had achieved their objective. They were inside the office under cover of their attack.

The element of surprise had given the outlaws

the advantage. The only slight consolation that David found in the situation was that the office was still in semi-darkness. This, combined with the smoke from the gunfire made it difficult to pinpoint the exact whereabouts of the outlaws even though they were only a few feet away.

David was aware that his heart was pounding like a steam engine. The outlaws would be bound to hear it and would know exactly where he was. But surprisingly the outlaws didn't seem to have heard it, since there were no bullets directed at him. The stillness continued. David guessed that when the next hail of bullets came there would be at least a couple of corpses joining Clint on the floor. Would one of them be his?

The silence was broken by the startling sound of glass breaking. There was a hail of bullets directed in the direction of the sound. Thankfully they were directed away from him and towards Al. The thought that Al had been hit was confirmed by a scream of pain. However, the shooting continued. David heard somebody fall and the unmistakable sound of another groaning and falling. He didn't have time to find out who since the blurred figure of one of the outlaws appeared a couple of yards in front of him. He pumped as many bullets as he could into him.

A few minutes later he surveyed the carnage.

The three outlaws were dead. He had been responsible for killing one of them. Al had killed the two others. In the process Al himself had also been killed. For several minutes the only sound in the office was of David being violently sick.

CHAPTER 29

Stan rode like the wind. He knew he had to reach the stage before the outlaws intercepted it. The one advantage he had was that dawn had not yet shown its face.

As he rode he thought about the last few hours he had spent with Marie. She had turned out to be a revelation – in more senses than one. She hadn't panicked during their escape from the cave. She had kept a cool head. Even helping him when he had been unconscious. True the relief of their escape from the jaws of death had proved too much for her in the end. She had been reduced to tears. This, however, had had its compensation in the form of their memorable love making. He prayed that he would be spared in the gun battle which was ahead so that he could return safe and sound to her.

He kept glancing at the sky. He thought he

could detect the first glimmer of light in the east. The outlaws would soon be breaking camp, if they hadn't done so already. He knew roughly where they intended to intercept the stagecoach. It was a gorge a few miles from Tom's cave. The stage would have to go through the gorge which was an ideal place for an ambush. The outlaws would probably arrive there during the next hour. They would take up their positions and wait. The stage would arrive, say, a couple of hours after sun-up – assuming it started from Hawkesville at dawn as planned. It wouldn't bother the outlaws that they would have to wait a couple of hours – they were used to waiting for the most suitable moment to rob a bank or train. More than that, they were used to waiting to come out when they been sentenced to a term in jail. He smiled grimly at the thought.

There was no doubt about it – the eastern sky was beginning to lighten. The outlaws would in all probability already be on the move. Although they would still be a couple of miles away, they would be able to see him if the sky lightened further. He knew he had to get past the gorge and head towards Hawkesville to intercept the stage before they spotted him. It was a race between him and daylight.

He had changed horses when he arrived at his

house. He had reasoned that the white stallion had worked hard enough in carrying two people on his back from the mine to the town. So he had hastily saddled a mare and was now riding her. She was a game horse who would keep going for hours if necessary. The only disadvantage was she wasn't as fast as the stallion. And at the moment he wanted as much speed as possible out of the horse.

The sky was definitely lightening. When he made that discovery he also found that he could see the gorge in the distance. He probably had a mile to go before he reached it. At that moment he was hit by another idea. Why not ambush the outlaws himself? He could hide up in the gorge. Then when they arrived he could pick them off. He was sure he would be able to kill a couple of them before they spotted him. The trouble was that there would still be three of them left. He hastily rejected the idea. That way he wouldn't have a hope in hell of returning to his beloved Marie.

He reached the gorge and galloped through it. He breathed a huge sigh of relief. At least he would be able to catch the stage before the outlaws ambushed it. The element of surprise would therefore be with him and whoever was on the stage.

In fact it took him another hour's riding

before he saw the stage in the distance. The sun was above the horizon and the stagecoach driver was able to see a solitary figure riding towards him. The man riding shotgun raised his rifle threateningly.

'It's all right,' said the driver. 'I can see he's got a sheriff's badge on.'

Stan rode up to the stage. Introductions followed. Stan discovered that a man named Ted Newbury, who was a representative of the stage company, was the only passenger. Ted explained his doubts about letting the consignment of money come on the stage without an escort.

'Well it's too late now,' said Stan. 'There are five outlaws waiting up ahead. This is what I suggest . . .'

An hour later the outlaws were happy to observe that the stage was on time. They scanned it eagerly for any signs of an escort. To their relief there was none. There wasn't even anybody riding shotgun.

'They're sitting ducks,' said Samson.

'We wait until they're opposite us before we ride out,' said Quail.

'Why don't we shoot the driver before we ride out?' demanded Carl.

'Because the horse will bolt,' Quail explained, patiently. 'We'll shoot the driver after we've grabbed the horses.'

Their plan went like clockwork. The five rode down from the rim of the gorge. They hadn't even bothered to split with two of them taking one side and three the other.

Quail fired his gun in his air to tell the driver to pull up. He did so with a stream of curses and in a cloud of dust. The dust helped to conceal the passengers from the outlaws. In fact it wasn't until it was too late that the five outlaws realized there were three men in the stage with deadly-looking guns pointing at them.

The first broadside from the stage killed three of the outlaws instantly. The other two, reacting to the devastating burst of fire, didn't hesitate. They swung their horses and headed in the direction from which the stage had come. Stan and the other two fired a few speculative shots after them, but the distance between them was now too great.

Stan examined the bodies. 'Quail and two of his accomplices,' he announced. 'He's the bastard I wanted to make sure of killing.'

Later, when he told Marie about the success of their gunfight, she said. 'I'm glad you've got Quail. I wouldn't have liked to have lived as your wife with the thought that he was still outside there somewhere.'

'Who says you're going to be my wife?' demanded Stan.

'You'd better say so,' said Marie. 'Otherwise what are we doing here, lying naked in your bed?'